D1576119

Legacy of Shadows

Legacy of
Shadows

Lillian Moats

DOWNERS GROVE,
ILLINOIS

THREE ARTS PRESS
1100 Maple Ave.
Downers Grove, IL 60515-4818

Publisher's Cataloging-in-Publication
(Provided by Quality Books, Inc.)

Moats, Lillian
    Legacy of shadows / by Lillian Moats. — 1st ed.
      p. cm.
    LCCN: 98-96937
    ISBN: 0-9669576-0-1
    1. Mothers and daughters—Fiction.   2. Mental
illness—Fiction.   I. Title.

PS3569.O6523L44 1999

                813'.54
                QBI98-990012

Printed in U.S.A. on acid free paper by Thomson-Shore
1 3 5 7 9 10 8 6 4 2
First Edition

Also by the Author

The Gate of Dreams,
a collection of stories for all ages
written and illustrated by
Lillian Somersaulter Moats

To obtain
Legacy of Shadows or
The Gate of Dreams,
contact your bookseller
or call:

THREE ARTS PRESS
(800) 777-2997

With love and thanks to these,
in order of their appearance in my life:
Chris, JP, Virginia, Michael and Dave;
and in grateful memory
of my parents' creativity
which instilled in me
what I most needed to survive.

Preface

Now that I stand in this sunlit clearing beyond a forest, menacing and deep, why do I want to take  your hand and walk again through these woods? Perhaps because I've found they can only threaten me if I try to leave them behind forever; and while I've learned to travel alone from light into darkness and back again, it would be lovely to have a companion now and then.

With these words as introduction I began, twelve years ago, to write a factual account of a desperate emotional breakdown—my own. Though it was well behind me, I hoped that probing its mysteries would protect me from a recurrence of the horrific symptoms which had seemed to strike from nowhere. As I reopened my past, I was overwhelmed by memories and startling insights. Eventually I came to understand that my illness had not been mine alone, but the inexorable culmination of a story set in motion with the death of my grandmother's two-and-a-half-year-old child, eight decades earlier. Stunned by this discovery, and torn by issues of accuracy and privacy in relating the lives of others, I put my writing aside.

But the story would not let me go. In exploring the particulars of my psychological history I had awakened, ironically, to its universality. Understanding the causes of my prolonged fragmentation ended my feeling of isolation, reconnecting me to the human family. I realized that the severity of my symptoms cast in high-relief a pervasive but illusive truth: that each of us is deeply directed by the legacy of unresolved emotion passed from generation to generation.

The book you are about to read is very different from my original attempt. Years after I abandoned my documentation, I approached the work as fiction, giving myself license, at last, to broaden the scope of the story beyond my own lifetime. I began to project myself empathically into the minds of the two women whose lives had funneled into mine, calling up images which might have captured their emotions at pivotal moments in their lives. A reader searching for the sensational will not find it in these pages; the story is not one of abuse, but of the best parental intentions gone awry—the most common of all human tragedies.

To release my unconscious understanding of an emotional legacy so deeply silent and encoded in symbol, I needed to call upon metaphor and meter. The resulting work is as much poetry as prose. Focusing on the interior lives and perceptions of a mother, daughter and granddaughter in turn, I adopted the format and intentions of the journal rather than the novel. As a granddaughter's transformation of family tragedy, *Legacy of Shadows* is an expression of faith that in our deepening self-knowledge lies the hope of liberation for ourselves and our children.

Lillian Moats
1999

Legacy of

Shadows

is the story of three women whose
psyches evolved, one from another.

Christianna Pemberty
1882–1919

Lisbet Pemberty Thomason
1905–1994

Anna Thomason
1946–

The tale is told in separate strands,
braided at the end.

BOOK ONE

Through Christianna's Eyes

Christianna Pemberty
1882–1919

Lincolnshire, England. November, 1904

The doctor's verdict has just been nailed outside our door: WHOOPING COUGH. I press my face against the glass to wail in silence. How can my child who, only twelve days past, conjured a menagerie in my lap, who roared and trumpeted, snarled and purred, nuzzled to be petted—how can she now lie torpid in her bed, in terror of the next spasm?

I rush back to her side. Oh, Anna, I am no child! Am I not twenty-two—old enough to mother you— old enough to save you? Have I grown up only to grow powerless? Her disbelieving eyes engage mine with a plea. They cannot comprehend I haven't the magic to transform her.

Dear God, could such a creature who, just twelve days past, ruled a wild kingdom from my lap, be vanquished at two-and-a-half?

II

Once Anna's eyes drew mine like magnets. Now they repel my gaze. I cannot look in them without blaming myself. Instead it is her hand on the rippled sheet, spread-fingered—like a little starfish—that attracts my soul.

Being a mother is all water and tides tonight. Each recurrent wave of her coughing engulfs us both. Yet it recedes only to drag her farther out to sea. I take her starfish-hand and hold it on my belly. I WANT TO GO WITH YOU, ANNA! If only the sphere under your hand were the moon; then the tide would pull you toward me.

But within this globe of my belly, your unborn sister or brother turns in its own salt-sea. And I must remain steadfast on this shore, torn in two.

Lincolnshire. February, 1905

The midwife says, "Quiet y'self, Mum—or you'll exhaust y'self before it's done."

I defiantly shake my head to signal, "Hush! I'll do this the only way I know." I cannot break rhythm without listing and fainting in the saddle. Father! If you were alive, you would understand—better than any midwife—that, giving birth, I am both wild horse and rider.

I train my eye hard upon the spire at chase's end and strain to clear hooves over fences and ditches. Every hurdle towers too high, stretches too wide as I approach. But I can refuse no obstacle. I set my jaw and ride, ride to the spire.

Didn't you tell me, Father, it breaks a horse's spirit to rein it in too hard at race's end? Even with a new life cradled in my arms, I gallop on, gripping the pillow between my knees. The contractions slow. I want to post homeward, gazing into the face of the tiny girl-child at my breast. But with the steeple behind me, I have lost all focus on my goal.

What materializes are the faces of the spectators, the devotees of the chase—my husband, the midwife, my sister. And though I look within myself to find you, there's no face so vivid as yours, Father.

What is your stern expression—a warning? I hear the other voices in one concordant hum, "The baby looks like Anna," they are saying, "exactly like Anna."

My heart clenches. The victory turns. Didn't you teach me to be loyal above all else, Father? I look down at this infant Lisbet, so ardent at my breast. Oh, Anna, she will never replace you!

Lincolnshire. January, 1907

Your third winter's come, Lisbet, and I can no longer contain you within the manger of my arms. I have become the shepherdess charged with your deliverance beyond the age when Anna died.

Poor lamb! I'm always at your back, tapping my shepherd's staff to the left, to the right of you to keep you true along this narrow pass of winter. You know nothing of seasons. You would spring and slide from this sheer slope—if it weren't for my crook at your neck and my stick clicking at your heels, driving you forward. You stop to bleat your tears, start to scramble backward to me.

I cannot let you, Lisbet. Every step for me is too painful to repeat. When you have survived this passage, will I allow myself to love you better?

I only know you're still retracing Anna's path, and that the day your footsteps take you beyond the end of hers is both the day I long for—and the one I dread.

Lincolnshire. February, 1910

"Please, Dear, it's been so long," you beg me. "Come watch me skate—you and the children." I swaddle little Martin until I fear he cannot breathe; and all the hazardous way to the lake, Love, I cling to you and Lisbet.

I know that as winter days go, this one glistens. I know that the sun ignites flares on the blades of your skates, that the sky is cerulean, that silver dust sprays from the prow of your feet as you stop to gaze at your son on my shoulder. I know that your figures are flawless, that you leap and land with weightless grace.

But you see that I see almost none of this. In these years since Anna died, your vantage point and mine have become misaligned. My sights have dropped to a hair's-breadth above the ground. I gauge the ice to be only a fine cold line between exhilaration and peril. I hover over its surface, magnifying fissures in its cross-hatched crust, detecting beneath it black water that waits.

The squeals of toddlers shatter my trance. Their parents don't even wrap them against the gouging wind. I want to tell every mother and father what I learned from Anna: *Life teeters on an edge as fine as the blade of a skate. Be dutiful to your children. Keep them warm.*

I temper my words. But I'm shunned for even the most delicate warning. The optimism of others terrifies me. Is it I, alone, who knows death is just a cold breath away?

I try to meet your eyes as you soar sunward. But you see me shut mine before I have to quake at the scrape of your landing, on the egg shell of the lake.

En Route from New York to Toronto. November, 1913

Steam swirls around the wheels, suspending our train in cloud, as we four hobble with our baggage along the platform. In eagerness for our new life, Lisbet has been coupled to me for months, like the tender-car behind its engine—fueling my dreams, keeping the fires of hope brightly stoked.

It is only November. Can it be Christmas morning? What New World elf has placed on every seat a bar of chocolate, wrapped in paper foil? We want to hoard our presents. But our hunger overrides our sentiment, and soon the gifts are only remembrance on our tongues.

Our Christmas story twists. The conductor comes to claim his due for every missing treat. Wise to the ruse, the other passengers snicker at our innocence.

My husband scrambles for our coins, so carefully allotted for meals between here and Toronto. Frail dreams dissolve like the steam clouds streaming past the window panes.

I nod at her drawing tablet, and Lisbet takes her cue to sketch the passing scenery. First one passenger, and then another jostles down the aisle and stops—astonished by her proficiency. I smile with pleasure, raising my eyes to the Americans for the first time.

Lisbet lifts her chin like mine, but goes too far, tossing her curls and flashing a look of self-satisfaction in my direction. This sort of attention must not be allowed to turn her head.

I vow that when we reach Toronto I will first unpack my copy book. My daughter needs to replicate the very page that was prescribed for me: *"Who shall stand in His holy place? He who hath clean hands, and a pure heart, who hath not lifted up his soul to vanity."*

For her own good, I disengage from my tender, yet curb her with my eyes. "Do not flash that look at me," they tell her. "Do not fancy yourself the most special child. Never forget there was one who came before you."

Toronto. March, 1919

I wake to find you bent over our bed, Love. I press your long fingers against my brow to trap their coolness, but their welcome chill warms on my hot temples. I push your hand away.

Every cough—no every breath—imbeds its blade more deeply in my chest. Did Anna feel these daggers when she died? You recollect a different sound—the yelp of her whooping cough. But when the razor cuts, I cannot tell if I am she or I.

I want to gather our children in my arms. No. I want to extend my arms' length and press our offspring to the farthest corners of this house to keep them safe. To think I've feared, in turn, each one would leave me—must I be the one to abandon them?

QUARANTINED. This morning, when the signs were pounded on our doors, I felt the nails, like irony, pierce my chest. It's a cruel prescription—that insures I won't infect the outside world, yet leaves the ones I long most to protect, entrapped with my contagion.

II

Days pass. Outside, the neighbor children press their faces to the glass, only to scatter at our slightest stir.

But it is I who hover long outside each aperture, pressing my face against the truth, peering inward at myself, at you and Martin, at Lisbet tending little Andrew and Ruth.

How many years, Love, has this house been stamped with my infection? I'm not referring to germs, for once, nor my influenza, nor the pneumonia to which it's turned.

I'm speaking of my *obsession*, my contagious fearfulness since Anna died. I can detect its shadow—but too late, I think—darkest at Lisbet's window, yet discernible through every chink.

III

My lungs are gorging with fluid, the doctor said. He doesn't know the kind. He cannot guess the years of swallowed sorrow you couldn't bear to see me shed. Even the coroner won't know it: death will be mine by drowning—my lungs only the last to be deluged in dammed up tears.

IV

After all the years of fearful caution, the sharpest pang of irony is this: I have, at last, no trepidation left of this disease—not for myself, not for you and the children. Time sorts our fates. It's too late for you to fall to this epidemic . . . too late for me to stand again.

Our bridal bed's become the one for birthing and dying. Oh, Love, after Anna, you should never have pressed me to conceive again.

If only, years ago, I could have thrown the sluice gates open . . . let my tears stream from every pore, cascade in rivulets down the bed-skirt to the floor, surge across a sodden rug, swell to the wainscoting, shatter the window panes, burst the doors, break our clandestine quarantine—that I might have infected everyone with just a tincture of my caution . . . and thereby spared those I've loved most, the paralyzing dose.

BOOK TWO

Through Lisbet's Eyes

Lisbet Pemberty Thomason
1905–1994

Toronto. March, 1919

They wouldn't let me visit you alone. At first, it was the germs that kept us out; then it was your frailty. Finally, when they filed the children past, we weren't allowed to speak—but only listen. So faintly that I had to read your lips, you whispered, "Lisbet . . . you'll have to be the little mother now." That's all.

Today the twins pulled Jack from his box. His mechanism's jammed. His handle's lost. And I'm thinking that I know what it is like to be a Jack-in-the-box. You huddle in the dark, unseen and not heard—until you catch the music racing at someone else's pace. Then POP!—you are on stage. I never minded, Mother, as long as I could feel your hand upon the crank.

Tonight I'm huddled in the dark with all my questions. I'll never know how fast or slow you'd have me go, or when to hide, or when to show. Today, they buried you inside a box, inside the ground, with all the answers.

Toronto. June, 1921

Sometimes I watch my hands as if they were not mine, as if they were not hands. Here at the sink they are birds' wings skimming the sudsy water, diving for their prey—a wooden spoon, a plate. The twins shriek like seagulls on either side of me, "More bubbles. Send more bubbles, Lisbet!" I swirl the froth and blow new bubbles gleaming down to Ruth and Drew. I wish that these were crystal balls, not bubbles, so I could steal a glimpse at what's to become of me.

You said you trusted that my hands would do

great works some day. But as you watched me twirling bobbins into lace, or catching a likeness in a sketch, you sometimes looked at my hands as if they frightened you. Did you see these hands as spirit wings—to carry me away? I'll never leave you, Mother. Don't be afraid.

I look down to find the dishes have all been done. The meager bubbles cower in the corners of the sink. My hands—no longer wings—slip round each other endlessly, wringing themselves, as if they weren't my hands at all, but yours.

Toronto. March, 1926

Painting beneath the skylights at the academy, I cast shadows. I stand out in three dimensions, don't I? It seems I amuse my professors. "She can capture anything we put in front of her," I've heard them say. "Everything's easy for Lisbet."

If only they could see me here at home where nothing's easy, and no one sees me. Martin's gone. The twins, grown discontent to be my dolls, have forged their own iron wills. And I lack my mother's skill to make them want to please me.

Father had me gather Mother's clothes to give away. And yet, he singled out one dress to keep. I puzzled at his choice: the slate gray woolen jersey— long sleeves, high neck, a deeply gathered skirt. It was neither the prettiest, nor Mother's favorite. Now, it hangs in her empty closet—like a woolen shadow.

Tonight, after my chores, I bent my head into Father's room to whisper goodnight. There he was, squeezing the shadow in his arms. I knew at once he'd picked the dress that could best enfold him, the one that could almost return his embrace. Father didn't see me waiting at his door. He'll never speak of this. And I will never dare to. The moment will be closeted with all the others we might have shared.

At the academy, I stand out in three dimensions,

don't I? But here at home, Father sees more of a person in Mother's empty dress than he has ever seen in me.

New York City. January, 1928

My hand plunging to paper, I find the quick of the model's pose, swing round his torso's curve, careen past his outstretched arm, brake for a change of direction, dart back to scribble the tautness of his buttocks, shoot down the zigzag of his leg—"STOP!" commands our drawing master.

While the model dreams up the thrust of his next pose, twenty-seven sheets of newsprint are ripped from their tablets and flipped to the other side. Begin again! By day's end the outpouring of drawings is stuffed into paint-smeared trash cans like stale headlines, so that only the experience survives.

Steering my portfolio into a snow-swept dusk, I absorb Manhattan through the art student's regimen of five- and ten-second gesture drawings. Every passerby is an artist's model. My drawing hand tenses—lunges—as if to scribble the indignant twirl of a skirt, the headlong dash to a bus, the fetal sleep of a drunk in a doorway, the downcast trudge through the slush.

Alone in New York, with no one to look after but myself, I'm emboldened. I feel the city's gestures as my own. My current flows, and I'm drawn into the scribble of this metropolis—more at home with all its verve, and power, and nerve, than anyone will ever know.

Toronto. June, 1929

Now that his household's grown disordered, Father's called me home. How could so much have changed while I was gone? Martin's here from California with a bride. My room's just one of theirs. They've claimed nearly the whole upstairs. And Father stands aside.

Martin calls me obstinate. "You'll have to dispose of all this artwork. We haven't room to store it. What, in God's name, are you saving it for?"

Obstinate. That was Mother's word for me. It hasn't lost its bite. And so, I gathered everything—I don't know what came over me—everything . . . from all the years at the academy, the latest from New York.

Martin and Emily, Father, Ruth and Drew—they watched me haul it by the armload down the stairs. They knew that I was dragging it out back to burn. And no one—no one stopped me.

I moved like an automaton, felt nothing till I saw my life ignite. I grabbed a board and tried to squelch the blaze. But every time I struck, I only split the monster's flaming tongues in two, so that its hunger multiplied. Then I stood back to die. I watched the landscapes scorch, the still lifes cringe before they curled. I saw the alchemy of cobalt flares shoot from the oils before the faces crawled. And when I glimpsed the one survivor at my feet—the sculpted likeness of myself—I grabbed it by its hollow throat and smashed it on the bricks.

Now that everything is ash and rubble, tell me this: if I had said, "I'm going to the yard to end my life," would anyone have stopped me?

II

Mother, I know I never shone like Anna in your eyes. But why do your other children look at me as if I were The Ash Girl, who never knew her place? If I leave, they resent me for trying to become more than they. If I stay, they resent me for being less than you. I can't find my way.

They never knew you as I did. They never knew the fairy tales we shared. You were my Cinderella, who cried in shame for those months when we first arrived in the Provinces; my Cinderella for the clandestine days when you scrubbed other people's dishes, clothing, floors, to feed Martin and me. You swore me to secrecy.

Now I've become Cinderella. I'm sure my grief for you has been as great as hers for her mother. Why is there no magic hazel tree above your grave to flourish from my tears? Where is the small white bird to shower down upon me what I need from you?

I'll never know where you might have stood the night I burned my life. I only know you would have made a plea for familial peace—at any cost. And so, I've made my truce, mended the split between my will and yours. Today I signed a contract with Lisador to serve as a promise to myself: I'll teach under his direction at the Young People's Art Center of the Academy. From this day on, I'll be only an inspiration to children, shun the spotlight, work behind stage. I'll threaten no one with my talent.

Now your family will be at peace, Mother. As for

the price? A sip from Cinderella's battered cup—the metallic aftertaste of swallowed pride.

Toronto. August, 1936

As I passed by on the way to the children's opening, her chauffeur swept a soft cloth—a bit of torn sail perhaps?—over her Rolls Royce, as if her car were the replica of a proud ship moored to the curb out-side the academy. Lisador had not told me Mrs. Taite was traveling from the States.

She hovered over the exhibition. Then, with her white gloves folded in her lap, she listened as I told her how I love to set the children free, turn their hands to wings. Mrs. Taite smiled, "You're the end of my odyssey." She promises to clear every impediment from my path, so I can "perform this miracle with children in New York."

Mother, I told her yes. I didn't ask for Father's

blessing. A chance like this may never come again. Didn't you depend upon my "gifts" to lift you in the eyes of strangers? Didn't you dream of palaces and balls? How can I fulfill those dreams of yours if I remain at home among the ashes?

Before Mrs. Taite left, her chauffeur leaned over the Rolls Royce. His gloved hand buffed the side view mirror, until the sunlight dazzled me—until I saw you, not her, standing next to me, dressed as you used to dream, in tasteful elegance, her gold broach fastening a collar of Belgian lace beneath your chin. Don't be frightened, Mother. She's only my patron: you're my patron saint.

New York City. May, 1940

At Rumplemeyer's after the symphony, he always orders a glass of Grand Marnier, and I, a concoction of ice cream. He draws me toward him with his stories, while he sketches on his rumpled program: pediments and friezes, posts and lintels, cantilevered forms, with his restless hand.

When he was only twenty-five, he came from England to design the Taites' estate—first hint of his shining armor. Does he court me on a white steed? Not quite. But he's a wonderful horseman, Mother. At five each morning his houseman wakens him with the announcement that a horse is ready at the hitching post outside the cottage door. Then Marcus rides the day in, before he rides the train into New York.

The night we met, he told me haltingly that he'd been married once, unhappily, years before. Surely you'd forgive him one mistake! Since his divorce, he's spent his leisure time adventuring with favorite cronies, fox hunting weekend mornings; spent summers sailing along the coast of Maine.

By now, I feel I've shared in all his past adventures, sailed beside him; ballooned above a shimmering river, trailing our own imposing shadow over the Connecticut countryside.

New York City. April, 1941

The children's creations staggered my audience. But in turn, the questions confounded me. Lisador once said I was "the master gardener, who enlivened the walls of the academy with the espaliered blooms of children's art." But I can't answer questions like these: "Miss Pemberty, how do you know what to do, what to say to inspire the children?"

Must I count words like seeds, gauge the breeze that carries them aloft, calculate the times I turn the soil, so I can prescribe for educators the flowering of children's art?

I could not tell them that, as teachers, their questions seem plodding; that, as gardeners, their feet seem mired in clay. Why do they stand upright, peering down at the seedlings, waiting for them to reach full height? Don't they understand the importance of kneeling in a garden—of joyfully kneading the soil?

I closed, instead, by saying that I have to follow my instincts, that I find it difficult to put these things into words. And still the applause was thunderous, Mother, like a sudden summer downpour that the soil can't absorb.

Above the tumult, then, I heard your voice remind me: *"Who shall stand in His holy place? He who hath clean hands and a pure heart, who hath not lifted up his soul to vanity."*

Willow Lane, Fairfield, Connecticut. September, 1942

Illusionist! He conjured up a dashing portrait of himself, implying all the while that after we were married I would be painted into it, depicted in all his adventures. But that was never his intent.

No more bright nights. They were only the rhinestoned lining on an indigo cape he tossed with such panache across my cityscape. He's snatched the drape away. Now I stand before a tangled country landscape. No more White Knight.

Through our picture window I see a forgery of Corot, just a foil for Marcus' brilliant strokes—twelve cadmium red coats. The fox hunters gallop across the hollow of our property. He canters into view, and like a fool I thrust out my hand to wave. It only thumps against our window pane like a bird tricked by reflections.

So much lay cloaked behind rhinestone and indigo: his terror of being seen as less than manly in the eyes of men, his mercurial temper. I glance down at the ring that we designed together. How has he turned diamonds and platinum into tears and quicksilver on my hand?

Only at Children's Place am I still visible—until at 6:18 each evening I meet Marcus aboard the home bound train. The car lurches into motion. And the silk scarf he used to swirl about my neck tightens into a tourniquet, cutting me off from the pulse of the city, from the rhythm of my own life.

Willow Lane, Fairfield. May, 1944

I startle at the prolonged "c–r–ack" of wood ripping in the near distance, and look up from our perennials to find Marcus splitting rails—as if nothing had happened. I kneel by the flower bed, trowel in hand, but still I haven't left the breakfast table. I can't stop reliving our conversation: "Don't you think it's time we had a child?" With these words he drives a wedge into me, rendering me open, incredulous.

"Isn't it too late for us? I'm thirty-nine, you're . . . . What about Children's Place and Helena Taite?" I stammer. "I couldn't give them up!"

He lets the weight of his hammer pound the

wedge home: "I would have thought you'd want to care for your own child. But that's between you and your conscience." He watches me rip along my core, both halves dropping at his feet.

New York City. December, 1945

"With you retiring from the helm," said Helena, "I haven't the courage for uncharted waters. It's time to close the doors of Children's Place forever, so we'll be remembered by our grand success." Now I'm alone with the easels, the looms, the jars of glaze, the reverberations of the children's voices.

I fold the ladder Jasper always climbed to create his murals. The boy applied his paint in layers, fashioning every detail of the aircraft carriers, the planes, from the inside out—never a gauge misplaced, never an engine missing a working part. And then, without a pause, he'd paint the metal hull over each master work, concealing it from all eyes, for all time.

The first time, it was hard not to stop his hand—until I realized the painting's meaning to him lay in what he would always know to be hidden inside. Each mural, I regarded as an innocent tribute to the boy's father, a fighter pilot who died over Stuttgart.

I have become both Jasper and his art. The self that others see—merely a layer of paint concealing my absorption with what lies hidden in me: the infant growing in my womb, my own strange visions, the awesome accountability for another soul contained in the hull of my body.

I mustn't stay here longing for my students. I remember, Mother, that when you were pregnant with the twins, you used to tell me how you held a constant vigil over your innermost thoughts—in order to protect the babies. I didn't grasp your meaning then. Now, even my sadness feels dangerous.

I try to lift my spirits, but I find only one consolation: if I can steady my hand during the under-painting, my child-to-be could be my finest work of art.

Hartford, Connecticut. January, 1946

When we were courting, he whispered breathlessly against the nape of my neck, "If you were ever ill, I could never bear to leave your bedside." Now I'm informed by the radium dial, which seems to vibrate in the blackness, that the night has almost passed—and Marcus will be breakfasting with friends before the hunt. At least the other expectant fathers pace in the waiting room nearby.

"How far we've come," the doctors say. But I refused their anesthetics, Mother, since you had none. The chief nurse could not hide her disgust—turned out the light, and left me laboring alone. I haven't seen a soul for hours.

The isolation, the darkness filled with lurching pain—was it like this for you? NO. It was not like this. When the twins were born, Father, Aunt Edna, the midwife—even I—hovered about your sun-filled room.

My anger swells with each contraction, until I think it's poisoning the fluid in my womb. I curl protectively around the bulge to shield my baby with myself—from myself.

The obstetrician bursts onto the scene, alarmed to find that I've been left alone—dumbstruck that I've begun to expel the baby on my own. The room floods with fluorescent light. But it recedes to one small point. Then everything goes blank . . . .

A smack—a cry! My eyes flash wide. Two images pulsate wildly: the doctor grasping my tiny, blood-smeared daughter by her ankles; and horsemen—the all too familiar snapshot of Marcus flaunting the coveted "mask" of the fox by its freshly severed neck.

The nurse sweeps my daughter past my eyes, wrapped in a snow white blanket, then whisks her to the nursery to be viewed behind glass.

If my rage has poisoning power, let it be to fortify my child with the antigens of anger. Didn't Thetis dip her infant headfirst in the River of Death to steel him? I'll teach my daughter about the wiles of men intent on the chase. Let her be as inscrutable as Achilles dressed in girlish clothes. Let her be more wary than a fox!

Willow Lane, Fairfield. February, 1946

The strand that fastened my daughter to me in the womb, though now unseen, is no less binding. I've named her "Anna" to make an unending circle of our loyalties. There is no border between my child and me. No boundary. At last, Mother—I have *my* Anna.

Willow Lane, Fairfield. October, 1946

Nine months old and she's walking! Like every other object in her path, I'm undone by this elf-child Anna. Where she's gone no lock has kept its key, no box its lid; and what she seeks, she always finds within—the rapture of revelation. I try not to mirror her puckish face, but she makes me laugh. She makes me live again!

Sarasota, Florida. March, 1947

Red Tide. The Gulf of Mexico is stained with a deadly bloom of plankton, like burnt sienna swirled with turpentine. The fish wash up on shore, their bodies torn, their gills gaping. I stare out of a rain-streaked window at an abandoned boat, while Marcus stalks the concierge for news of accommodations on the Eastern coast.

Leaving Anna was the hardest thing I've ever

done. She's the element in which I live and breathe. Without her, every fiber of my being rips.

"We'll only be gone a fortnight," Marcus scoffed, pressing his demand on me. "After two or three days, she won't even remember you."

What can a man know about a daughter's grief? Anna must think I'm gone forever—severed from her, the way you were from me, Mother. How overjoyed she'll be to have me home again. What does Marcus know about our chain of loyalty?

Willow Lane, Fairfield. March, 1947

Longing for our reunion, I got down on my knees to greet her—on my knees! What sort of creature evades her mother's embrace, runs on staggering legs to a hired nursemaid? Marcus reveled in his vindication— parodied my humiliation to the roaring laughter of the maid.

MOTHER! I've clung to the memory of your love my whole life long! What sort of daughter can this be who trades her loyalty in two short weeks? Nothing will ever be the same between this changeling child and me. Nothing. If I ever knew my Anna, this can't be she!

II

Now that morning's come, the stranger climbs out of Anna's crib to totter toward me—her pajamaed feet slapping on the maple flooring. Her prodigious eyes peer up at me, laboring to read my face. But I won't allow it. I turn on my heel and walk away—faster than she can follow.

Gray Street, Fairfield. December, 1947

When I watch her clutching two crayons in each hand, humming over her pictures, I forget to be wary of her. "How like I was," I say repeatedly. How like I was in every way—except her mutability.

Gray Street, Fairfield. March, 1948

The doctor's left, and left me quaking. *Now* who is this child who lies delirious in Anna's bed; who does not know me, yet clutches my fingers like two crayons? Who is this child whose forehead broils, who coughs as if she would turn her little body inside out?

Oh, why did I ever name her "Anna"? Does she languish as your Anna must have done—and nearly at her age—just to torment me? I've never been so terrified.

Here at the kitchen sink my hands assume your fervor on their own. They won't stop scouring until every germ is drowned in scalding water, every threat is poisoned in soap. I won't stop scouring until I find a tracery of your blood in the cracks of my knuckles. There's nothing I wouldn't do to save our child.

II

Buried under the bedclothes here on the couch, my face to the winter window, my back shielding my child, I'm afraid to move, Mother. PNEUMONIA! I'm petrified I'll die from it, like you—only to leave my daughter humming by my bedside. "You brought this on yourself," the doctor told me, "nursing Anna back to health."

A sharp breath pierces my lungs. Mother, they said you felt these daggers when you died. I hear a noise and call, "Is that you, Dear, on the stairs? Is that you in the kitchen, Anna? Promise you won't get into the knives!" She appears instantly to reproach me with her eyes.

Outside the window . . . the snowfall scumbles the blank sky to create . . . the final layer of gesso. Is my canvas ready, then? Into my dream again . . . drifting toward her . . . always Anna . . . a portrait of Anna. I paint it from the photo of her on your dresser, Mother.

My sleep-laden lashes flutter down my picture. The portrait blurs, so much reworked . . . features glare . . . layer to layer. "Just like yours," they tell me. Everyone tells me, "Her eyes are just like yours." But they couldn't be like mine . . . Anna died before I was born! I dab with fury! Stabbing the air, my hands waken me.

Flinching, I find . . . ? Who watches over me with disapproving eyes . . . Anna? Anna? *Christianna!* Please, not so harshly, Mother—hold me tenderly in your eyes!

III

I hear her humming near me. "Don't leave my bedside, Dear," I say, "you'll worry me." I strain to sit. She clambers onto the couch to try to lift me, reaching above her head to pat my cheek. "Mama's sad again," she states.

She scrambles into my lap, and I feel a floodgate open at my depths. I turn a tear-streaked face away. "Mustn't tell . . ." a whisper surges over my tongue, "mustn't tell anyone I spoke to you like this. I haven't a soul to talk to!"

Decades of passion rise, churn into words and break in a torrent. "Anna," I hear myself whisper, "you'll have to be my little mother now . . . ."

BOOK THREE

Through Anna's Eyes

Anna Thomason
1946–

Part One
(1957-1966)

Ravine Road, Fairfield. December, 1957

My baby dolls were always real to me. Suddenly, it bothers me to see their eyelids painted on their eyes. I don't like the sound of their lashes—like tiny straight combs—clacking against their cheeks. How could something that has no feelings, have seemed so sweet to me?

Now that I'm too old for dolls and too young for babies, my mother's angry with me for growing up. I know she is! She says, "You'll be wanting to leave me soon, Anna." And she blinks her eyelids—hard—to clear the tears.

"I'm only eleven," I have to remind her, as I reach out my hand to comfort her. But she turns and walks away, and doesn't see—I'm not the one who's leaving.

Fairfield. April, 1959

Ever since he taught me how to dance The Charleston, Father and I have nothing to say when we pass in the hall. We just sing, *"Dot-dah, dot-dah, dot-dah-dah-dah, dot-dah."* Like metronomes turned up-side-down our straight arms swing the tempo from our shoulders. Our legs, tight down to the knees, go wild below—one pointed toe and then another flicking thigh-high. We jump and cross our feet mid-air, then twirl so that we're face to face again, to back away. With a zigzag twisting of our soles we press a diamond pattern on the rug, and wave good-bye to one another, with five pointed fingers on our tick-tock hands.

A spring rain, like the mist from Mother's perfume atomizer, dampens my cheeks as I leave my country school. I put my arm around my cello's back, and grasp the leather strap of its canvas raincoat, so we can stroll home hip to hip.

Now that I've finally learned to whistle, I just whistle "Singin' in the Rain"—but the words go soaring through my head. I keep my eye on the curve of the road ahead. And when there are no cars in sight, I secretly get "dancing feet," as Father calls them.

Today it's not The Charleston that propels them; it's something smoother. I dip and sway and twirl around and around with my cello, until the point of his metal foot lifts high in the air, and he nuzzles his damp neck against my shoulder.

Ravine Road, Fairfield. August, 1959

In June my mother told me, secretly, that Father had been married once before. It was nothing to me. I bounced a little ball and caught her secret for her as easily as a jack in my hand, and barely felt it while I held it there for her. But that was only the first round. And it's always Mother's turn to toss the jacks.

Now it's August, and I pick up her bitter hurts in two's, three's, five's at a single beat. She's scattered more secrets than anyone could gather at a sweep— more, I think, than even a grown-up hand could hold. They pierce their points into my palm as I try to hide them for her.

Has she forgotten that her husband is my father? She remembers every injury. They cling to her like burs. She waits till we're alone so she can pluck them off, and toss them my way.

Fairfield. October, 1959

I watch the fog begin to rise on the windshield from her sobbing. And I think about the quiz show host explaining how the temperature and flow of air is regulated for the contestants, who strain for answers in their glass booths. Not here! It seems there's only enough air for one of us to breathe.

Oh, Father, I will tell you in my heart what I must never tell you. All autumn long she's been driving me to one secluded lane after another, so no one will discover she's confiding in me. The car's become our isolation booth to keep the world away. And now she waits for my reply.

"Loyalty." She's only asking for my loyalty. And yet the word leaps from her lips, Father, to tear at my throat. I know she's asking me to choose between the two of you. And I can feel her dying for my answer.

Minutes slide. I watch the rivers ripple down the inside of the windshield. What am I waiting for? If only once I had seen a tear glimmer in your eye, Father; then there might have been a contest. But Mother needs me. And you, it seems, need no one.

I kiss her tear-stained face in answer, and beg her silently to take me home. And I wonder how, my whole life long, I'll manage to tell you with my eyes what I must never tell you.

Ravine Road, Fairfield. September, 1961

It was your whirring bobbin that called me to you as you wove. I was so small that I could peer through the open threads above my head to watch the blur of your shuttle as it flew between your hands. I would sway to the sure measures of your pedals until my feet danced away from you, keeping your rhythm.

How I wished, then, that I could sit beside you, Mother, like weavers do at double looms. They toss their shuttles back and forth to one another, advancing their cloth like dialogue—one delivering his line, the other catching it, and answering in kind. But now that I'm as tall as you, I've been apprenticed to your brain. We weave our frantic conversations side by side on a phantom loom, here at the breakfast table before school. You toss your shuttle to me, its bobbin wound in thought, setting the rhythm of our talk, plotting the pattern of our day—what tasks to undertake, amends to make, what cautions to obey. We weave the cloth to cloak our imperfection, now that Father expects not just a perfect wife, but also a flawless daughter.

"Remind me, Dear, to . . . after school to . . . . Mustn't forget . . . . Remind me, won't you?" I have only seconds to repair your strand of thought, splice broken words, untangle your meaning, shuttle it back for confirmation—before you snatch the beater from me, change the pedal, alternate the threads.

"Check to make certain, Dear, that . . . I've . . . in the basement . . . . Please—go now and check." I leave the table, dash down the basement stairs—guessing it's the iron you want unplugged, like yesterday—and hurry back again.

". . . you know . . . to . . . what's her name? Don't say a word about . . . . I'd die."

I can't bear your urgency. "Wait, Mother! I can't follow you," I say. You glower. I've thrown you off your pace. Your rhythms syncopate. With hands and

feet working at cross purposes, you shuttle instructions to me in volleys now, bobbins snapping, jam-
ming, catching in reversing threads.

We are two tricksters from a fairy tale gone
wrong. We weave the cloth to fool our emperor. But
only you believe our craft invisible. Father looks up
from his paper. My eyes plead, "Only you can stop
us." But he can't listen any longer to the madness of
our talk. He clenches his jaw, and does what I must
never do: he walks away.

Fairfield. July, 1962

Like a spark tossed to the present from the Renais-
sance, De Santos alights on the step of his studio, then
vanishes—instructions given. His spirit lingers for an
instant, then dissipates. I'm left grinding pigments for
him on a marble slab.

I prefer the days we work together on his murals,
but I'll absorb the ancient ways however he pre-

scribes. I weigh the powdered pigment, dull and dry, and place it on the ivory stone. I think about the privilege of knowledge handed down, and picture you alone at home. Why do you work only at crafts, and leave the arts to me, Mother? You who are far more talented than I.

I count the drops of linseed oil I add. Each liquid lens brightens, magnifies the Persian red. If it caught a ray of sun, I think it would ignite in fire.

I would have stopped you, Mother! I would have crushed the match, and never let you set your work ablaze. What's more—I would have dissuaded you from closing Children's Place. The eager students left behind, the ones who never had a chance to come— because I came instead—they haunt me, every one.

I take the muller in my hand and swirl it to blend the pigment with the oil. I scrape the slab, amass the colored paste and grind twice more to twenty-five.

De Santos performs the master's test. Smearing a dab of paint across clear glass, he holds it to the sun.

"Your particles have not yet intimately mixed throughout the oil," he says.

But it is you I picture, Mother, testing *our* oneness. You hold a sample to the light and say, "Your attributes are too distinct from mine."

I know I've failed you. I'm insoluble in mother-love. But when I find my medium, I'll dissolve in love, prove to you that I can blend! I'll make an art of love—never forgetting what you've taught me. What you've needed, Mother, and I've failed to give, will be like De Santos' standard held to the sun. Let my love outshine his paint like stained glass fused in fire!

Fairfield. October, 1963

Brent looks directly through me with his love—the same way Father does—so that I have to look away. He breathes my name urgently, "Anna . . . Anna . . ." and I know who I am—apart from everyone—and that, itself, seems wrong.

But worse . . . in another season, another woods, before these leaves unfurled—didn't I make promises to Peter? Didn't I swear I'd be true while he's away at Amherst, never kiss another? Six months passed without a breach. Now the woods are strewn with broken promises like fragments of stained glass.

Isn't it a fellow artisan, though, who stirs his chemistry in me . . . whose kisses heat my lips, my temples, the hollow of my neck, melding our colors indelibly?

There are only days before Peter returns. I tremble from wanting Brent, bury my face in my hands. He kisses my tears. "I'm glad you're crying," he confesses. "It means at least there's hope for me." He'll wait for my answer. What will it be?

Ravine Road, Fairfield. November, 1963

Haltingly, over the phone, I hear myself say, "I have to stop seeing you . . ."

First—a boundless silence, then—"Can I come to

say good-bye?" There's an edge to Brent's voice, sharp enough to score my heart. He doesn't need his artful hand at all. And still he uses it to grip mine as we take a final walk into our ravine.

Suddenly he skims me off my feet, then sets me down again on a fallen tree to kiss me, passionately—here, below my heart—at my very center. I hold his head against my chest.

"I'm going to miss you so much . . ." The words start from our lips in unison. We have to turn our backs on one another to tear ourselves away. I run home—leaves crunching like glass under my feet.

II

What a price I've paid to prove I can be true in love. I can't believe I've let him go! I stare through the living room window at the curtain of snow descending over our ravine.

As soon as I press my hand on the pang where Brent's final kiss remains, an impulse strikes my infidelity—like a wordless thought, but more invincible than thought—like a shock, but more electrifying! I tear my eyes from the snowy window, and am stunned to find them in the mirror above the bathroom sink, flashing as green as Mother's. They don't want to meet my gaze, are drawn instead to my own hands washing themselves, as if they weren't my hands at all.

How disobedient is my love—how obedient my loyalty.

New York City. December, 1964

Glitter is sifted in front of a blackened sky. The snowfall softens the "whoosh" of traffic on Riverside Drive, muffles the shriek of subway brakes at 116th and Broadway, so it can whisper to me, privately.

Because I hear it as a kind of calling, I can't do otherwise than to step away from my friends, forego a round or two of sliding on our pilfered cafeteria trays, down the icy incline behind the Barnard dorms.

But what is the meaning of the snow that beckons me? I can't trace its power, yet I feel relieved that I can work it out as memory; unlike the words I hear these days that no one ever spoke, unlike the sights that disappear on second glance. More than a year must have passed, since that first snow last winter whitened—widened—the ravine between my senses and myself.

Feeling a tug on my gloved hand, I join my men and women friends again. Away from home, at last, and therefore liberated to be children, they make a throne of intertwining hands for me.

I can't believe how unobservant others are—new friends and old—that they still think of me as whole, that they assume that my perceptions work like theirs, that they believe they know me, and still think they love me.

New York City. January, 1965

I suppose this little elevator must have had an operator once—and that it misses him or her so much it's lost its mind. Poor little automaton, ferrying us carrel-ers among the stacks. It remembers its routines but not its reason—remembers how, but cannot think of why.

It ascends to an appointed floor; but no longer having a mind for precise callings, it adds one—more or less—perhaps a half, three quarters. Then, convinced of a vision of would-be passengers, it opens its steel gates perfunctorily onto a blank brick wall—closes and opens them again in seamless sweeps, like an accordion playing itself.

It shuttles down from six-and-a-half, halts tentatively to display our feet at eye level to those waiting on five—catches its error—descends for a correction, before parting its gates with conviction, to divulge our faces to the ankles of groaning students on four.

When, at last, the fractional errors compound to make a whole, the other travelers gladly escape. My public self gets off with them, quipping and laughing, but my private self holds out for number seven. I'm alone on board as the steel bars close in front of me. My smile writhes into a quivering chin.

I could scramble out at the next opening, run down the fire stairs, phone Peter, arrange to meet him at Princeton this weekend. I could hop on the subway, have a milk shake at Rumplemeyer's, stay downtown for the symphony. I could escape this maddening elevator—as if it would make a difference to one who travels everywhere inside a roving, raving cell.

Ravine Road, Fairfield. March, 1965

Breaking a promise to myself, I've shown her the skin scrubbed blood red over my knuckles, enumerated the endless rituals, detailed my visions, recounted the imagined sounds. How I had feared we would begin to merge again, if ever I betrayed my symptoms to her.

But, as if a swatch of window screen had insinu-ated itself between us, her face dims, then darkens. Her mouth hardens before she responds. "You'll never suffer a pain I haven't had to endure and more. You'll just have to live with it, like me."

"Then I'm not as strong as you, Mother, I'm going INSANE!" I scream. Her focus shifts to the wire screen inches before her eyes, as I blur beyond her recognition.

I drop to my knees in front of her, "Please, Mother, let me get some help!"

"Think of someone else for a change," she com-mands, "and stop being dramatic!"

I pick myself up from the floor—struck dumb that I've become the stranger. She has slammed her shutters and bolted her door.

II

Viewed from the cold, gray sky of my ceiling, my

bedroom walls are as stark and confining as the cement container of a canal lock. I stare down at a small boat afloat in frigid waters.

Its sails have been lowered, bundled into strait-jackets—its moorings stretched taut to prevent it from ramming its wooden sides. It only waivers slightly at the echoed clang of the lock's steel gates.

The cement walls elongate gradually, extending stories below me, as the waters slowly drain from the lock. The silence is so profound that when the out-going steel gates spread their arms there is hardly a rushing sound.

There can be no backward turning. Unbound, the boat slides out into deeper waters, heading—without a captain—for the open sea.

Ann Arbor, Michigan. July, 1965

Leaving the art school, I am as resolute and clear this summer night as the North Star, ardent above me.

There are times like this, to be sure, when I can override my illness to listen to my wiser self. Without another soul in sight, I cut across the quadrangle toward the dorms, counting my mistakes.

I shouldn't have broken off with Peter. But I was so tired of being preserved between the leaves of a book—this time, while he's in London, having his adventures. And when Mark said, "I've kept you in my sights all summer," I was flattered to be hunted, fell in love—not with the hunter, I'm afraid—but with the sureness of his aim. Since I've been proud to think that I could spot the tender traits in any man, it hurts me to admit how I mistook him.

The marksman felled his prey, but found the deer he stunned to be less seasoned than he'd thought. Running his sinewy hand over the hide, he spied the markings of a fawn, read lingering spots of innocence to be emblems of affluence—a trait he hates—and hates himself for being attracted to. He won't unfasten the ties, but he'll insure his dear's no longer fawned over. While he waits for my spots to fade, he toughens me with piercing jabs he thinks his duty to inflict.

When I went to him tonight to say he didn't need to walk me home, how drawn he was to the defiance in my eye. And yet, I think I saw him check the snare, in case his lines were fraying.

II

All it will take to break away is to admit to my mistake—without a hint of hesitation. Tomorrow's the day. Without a person anywhere in sight, I leave the quadrangle, still resolute and clear—until a huge arm—white in the moonlight—lunges for me from behind a shrub!

The man, half naked, bolts to block my path—I dodge and run across the grass. Feeling his shadow stretching to reach me, I veer between buildings. The pavement whizzes underneath my feet until I wonder if the ringing footsteps still are his, or just the echo of my own inside a marble archway. I turn to find him gone, and still I cannot slow my pace.

Breathless, I finally overtake another soul, and ask if I can walk beside her to the women's dormitories on the hill. She turns to me. There's not a shred of common feeling in her eyes. And when I tell her what I'm running from she looks away—granite hard and disbelieving. I drop back to let her get ahead of me, more lonely now than if I'd never come upon her.

For months, I've been pursued by visions mad as Hieronymous Bosch: transparencies projected from my mother's caveats. She paints impressions of the world of men, and then—as if she telegraphs her pictures to my brain—our endless, one-way conversations live anew. As fast as I can paint them out they bleed through again, like lurid underpaintings.

Although I know that what took place just moments past was not a vision—hers or mine—I fear, when I'm alone inside my single room, my brain will tamper with reality. Once a moment's passed, its memory's fair game for my dismantling.

By morning, will I renounce what meager trust I have left in my perceptions—name the man an apparition, after all? Or, will I conclude that—since he did lunge out at me—I invited it, and that this incident is only one of many I've repressed?

I stop dead on the overpass to gape at the dorm lights stacked upon the hill ahead. A scream as deafening and mute as that immortalized by Edvard Munch distorts my face. I can't make it through this night alone. I must call someone—whom? The dime I've found among the crumbs in my poncho lining . . . will it help me reach my parents, somewhere in the isles of Greece? Peter in London? Even if it could, I can't crawl back to them. I have no women friends on campus yet. I cross the overpass and step inside the street-side booth.

I take a wavering breath and dial Mark. But when he answers, I can make no sound at all. I'd been as resolute and clear as the North Star, ardent above me.

III

He tucks me snugly in his bed, insisting that he'll stay awake all night, in case my dreams should frighten me. Is Mark, after all, the man I once thought him to be? Clutching the vindication of first faith like a talisman at my breast, I try to dispel the horror of this evening, recalling something, not of Mark . . . but Marcus.

Father lifts me lightly in his arms, so I can watch him wind our grandfather clock. He opens the glass door at the top, restrains my stubby finger only slightly, as I point above the numerals to a little boat in the harbor, snug houses by the shore, a clock tower painted in the distant landscape.

Inspired by the rarity of this moment, Father shows me how the full moon in her lunette—smiling as mysteriously as the Mona Lisa—glides through her arc, until she disappears behind the sun. "Someone to watch over me . . ." he sings shyly, by way of tender explanation.

He then inserts the clock-keeper's key ceremoniously, twists it decisively, and sets me down. He lets me open the wooden door below, and with my fingertip, he sets the pendulum in motion.

• • •

Several times I startle in the night to find Mark lying next to me, keeping his vigil outside the covers, head propped on his arm. Each time, his kisses brush my forehead until I sail to sleep again.

When a cool breeze through the window makes me shudder, I open my eyes to find dawn quivering between night and day. Mark kisses my lips. "Anna, I've never felt this close to anyone before," he whispers. "Can't I finally make love to you?"

On my father's clock, the moon and sun face off between last night and a new day, advancing no time while I decide. But, somehow, the choice seems not about virginity.

As softly as the breeze, Mark breathes over my heart, unable to hear its pendulum swinging between poles. TLICK-TLOCK, faith in men—or fear of them. TLICK-TLOCK, love—or revulsion. TLICK-TLOCK, trust—or paranoia. TLICK-TLOCK! my self—or my mother! TLICK-TLOCK! sanity—or madness!

IV

I look no different, do I? Yet is anything the same? In this alien landscape of his rooftop—stranded between earth and sky—he proposes marriage to me. "Yes, of course," I comply with a sinking heart. I try to retrace the softness in his face I found at dawn this morning, try to recall his vigilance as love. But his looks at me have again altered.

Doesn't he eye me triumphantly, and yet suspiciously, as if I were a bride he'd plundered from an enemy? Having been rejected by those of means before, he abhors my family—swears allegiance to his state of poverty. If only he would trust me! Haven't I, too, felt cast out?

Now it dawns on me that he lives the life of a bitter exile—in an imagined nation under siege. I spy barbed wire at the horizon when his black eyes narrow—as if he were a border guard who draws a bead on me.

Not knowing it would be a dowry, I gave away what I'd never counted as treasure—my liberty. To be a virgin meant the far-flung provinces of love might still be visited. I never knew that, until today.

Ann Arbor. June, 1966

Where have I been this night of months since we were married? I imagine sawdust and peanut shells beneath my feet, the smell of grease, the creak of ramps that list and sway as he presses me through his maze, the shriek of a parrot jangling its cage, the cursing of lone, gruff voices—the carnival after hours.

Something's turned in me. He's gone too far, my secret husband. Now I gather sparks to ignite a lantern for my own escape. I wrestle my arm from his grasp, whirl with my lamp to see what sort of place I've been detained in longest. Light ricochets, flashes, coruscates from contorted glass—the House of Mirrors is where he's tested me.

"Do you still love me, wife, now that you've seen my soul's perversion?" How the King of the Carnival has relished the warp of his likeness in every glass! And how I've stretched and strained my love, to encompass him in all his guises.

My lantern's still too dim to find the way out. But he has seen the oath in my eyes, and he knows his reign of terror's nearly over.

Ann Arbor. September, 1966

I teeter on the median outside the courthouse clutching the papers in my hand—proof that a fawn can turn to vixen. Haven't I tricked my husband out of a marriage he began to cling to, once he was convinced I'd turned as cynical as he?

What's done is done. Then, can a marriage be erased like words on a chalkboard, dispersing in a chalk cloud with the clap of hands? The law says yes and, on a technicality, annuls our year-old union— only proving the absurdity of laws and vows.

What does one do just after a secret marriage has been secretly annulled? There's no one to go to, no one to tell. The wind, whirling behind a truck, blows me into the opposing lane. Death could be an answer—or a self-portrait. Sometimes they're the same.

I slump home to my easel, wondering through whose eyes I should depict myself today. Mark's? Then shall I paint myself as a traitor? Mother's? Then shall I paint myself as Mark? If, as she says, my face has taken on the treachery of his, shall I portray myself through my deceitful eyes, and paint a lie? I only know my painting should be dark.

No face appears against the background—only a word, "ANNULLED." What is it that has been rubbed out? The tenuous faith I had in my inherent goodness? My naive hopes for a family of my own? How could I bring children into a world as dark as this, as dark as I? It's not my past, but future that's been nullified.

Ann Arbor. November, 1966

The premature unfastening from life can go unnoticed even inwardly awhile. Then one awakens to find one's own hands delicately clipping.

Each strand, severed quietly and left to dangle, withers soon, and leaves no trace of its unraveling. Until one day, one sees so few connections. Disentanglement is all but done. What was once a web incalculable, is but a single knot.

When one is held here by so frail a tangle, either course looms full of pain. How can a web whose pattern's lost, now be rewoven? How shall a knot so vital be untied?

Part Two
(1967–1975)

Ann Arbor. April, 1967

Shall I rewrite a myth for us, Jean-Paul? I can, you know, with only a little tweaking, make it tell *our* opening. You, as Epimetheus, ignore Prometheus' warning never to accept a gift from Zeus and, trusting, take me gladly. Gladly, though I arrive clutching that chest, laden with secrets, heavy as lead.

It's not my curiosity but yours that makes me open it—not wanting you to invest yourself in a woman with a casket full of gods know what. If you are going to love me, you'd better know who I am. In my confessions, I lift the lid only a hairsbreadth at a time, knowing what plagues I might infect you with.

"You haven't scared me yet. What else do you have

in there?" Epimetheus smiles, unflinching. Pandora opens her wooden chest wider and wider to you.

Now a pandemic of wings and fins escapes the box, teeming, shrieking their pandemonium. You catch them in your finest net and, ignoring their crescendo as if it were only a well-worn recording of *Bolero* blaring in the background, you sit cross-legged in front of me, calmly sorting my demons, letting me test reality through your eyes.

"So . . . is that it?" asks Epimetheus, after days and weeks of this, tossing the last demon, like an empty cicada shell, over his shoulder.

Surely there must be more. I peer into the black box—detect a furtive fluttering of wings. "Aha!" I say, "I knew there'd be no end to it!" I grope for the illusive one, and catching it by the pinion, I hold it up for your inspection, looking beyond the beast to search your eyes. Epimetheus suddenly looks Pandora hard in the face. "I can't tell you what this is, if you don't know it."

She looks askance at the creature, then—as a test—plunges her other arm deep into the box, listens for her fingers thumping from empty corner to empty corner. Emboldened now, she confronts the last winged being, still dangling in her hand. "Name it," says Epimetheus, "only if you dare."

"I think I've heard them call this 'hope,'" Pandora answers, containing the creature. And she lies down next to Epimetheus, assured at last, that at least he knows what he is getting into.

Ann Arbor. May, 1967

I don't dance with you, Jean-Paul—you, the only member of the band who can't be spared for a single song. But when the thunder of your drums breaks through the threshold of my reticence, I do dance *for* you, peering through a burgeoning cloud of onlookers to stay coupled to your eyes.

In the safety of such connectedness you don't have to be perpetually entertaining, I don't have to be perpetually reserved. Our love's all rhythm and liquid vibes, as my body comes alive for yours.

Riding astride your old Yamaha, as close behind you as I can squeeze, I am always drenched—either from the outside-in, from hidden slits in the Naugahyde secreting reservoirs of rain—or from the inside-out, lush liquid summoned by a sensual buzz that does not quit when we dismount.

We spill up the stairs of your rooming house, peeling off helmets and whatever else can be loosened on the run, so we can slide into bed, without missing a beat of the rhythm—our rhythm.

Ann Arbor. September, 1967

He swims to the ocean's bedrock where I live and, ignoring the deep sea diver's maxim: *"never touch anything too beautiful or ugly"*—he touches everything

I am. So little sun has penetrated here these several years that I am fascinated, watching a ray illuminate his hand as he gropes at the boundaries of my watery darkness.

Within days we'll be married. I obey an urgency to tell Jean-Paul that—loving him—I feel a brightening at my depths. Perhaps I *can* imagine us with children. Suddenly his hand springs back from me! I quell my wavering thoughts. One marries for love—I tell myself—not hope of having children. And didn't he say he may have a change of heart someday?

I lie back to watch a ray of sunlight from the ocean's surface play in his waving hair as he twists and plunges through these depths. Nothing he finds is too profound for him to fathom. He touches everything I am.

Ann Arbor. October, 1967

The world is our cutting garden. At day's end, we bring to one another pluckings of life, like armloads

of flowers: a snippet of dialogue overheard, a carica-
ture scribbled on a napkin, an unwritten short story
lived that afternoon. We arrange the harvest in our
communal vase.

There is no otherness when we're together. So
disparate on the surface, so analogous at our cores—
we are each other's similes and metaphors.

Paris, France. October, 1968

A shared career has opened for us. To far-flung fes-
tivals we follow a film we wrote and animated
together. Chauffeur of our camper bus, Jean-Paul
has shown me how to enter foreign capitals without being absorbed into swarms of mini-cars. We
wait until the pre-dawn hours, when we can have a
city nearly to ourselves, and don't mind sharing it
with a handful of others. There is always a bounty
to go around, so—Jean-Paul claims the Pantheon, I
claim the slumbering Louvre.

With the October trees incandescent in the glow of street lamps, we park and stroll along the Seine until dawn. Before the face of Notre Dame he tells me, "Everything but the great bell was melted down during the Revolution . . . ." I'm distracted by his parted lips, and turn to kiss him, open as a bell. But he damps down the pealing of my heart—stopping our kiss short.

Oh, Jean-Paul, do you think I've not found out your shell game? You aim to substitute the lure of art and place in our hearts for high romance. The bell our passion tolls in you has begun to ring with a double tongue: euphoria—and terror that all things end in death.

Haven't I finally proven I can blend? Then what is this downward pull? Only months ago, weren't we magnets for each other's ardor? But in those fires, our mettle melted into one—and now, it seems, without opposing poles our oneness has become our gravity.

Madison, Wisconsin. March, 1971

With his arms around my waist, I hold the globe of Jean-Paul's head in my lap. Anguish streams from his eyes as he cries about the blackness—the "awful blackness" he had wanted never to have to share with me. But for him, the greater our success at breaking down our barriers, the more unbearable has grown the irony that, ultimately, we would die separately— leaving one of us to grieve inconsolably.

Brave Epimetheus so effortlessly dealt with Pandora's darkness, because it paled next to his own. Now he confesses that for several months he's been obsessed with the duty that—one day, in two consec- utive moments—he would need to kill us both!

• • •

There is no word, is there, for a double-suicide without consent? I watch my hands. One traces the curves of Jean-Paul's hair. The other still cradles the sphere of his head, as I realize that the immeasurable darkness of the universe is contained within this orb—along with all my stars.

Evanston, Illinois. August, 1973

By my transparent shock, I relieved Jean-Paul, for all time, of the awful duty that so appalled him. Now I'm the one who staggers on the precipice, peering at our fate. Let me die first—suddenly. Let oblivion snatch me, so I won't be the one to feel the awful tearing.

Yet, would I wish for Jean-Paul the fate I long to avoid? What if . . . what if . . . there *is* an afterlife. What if endless time, like a conveyor belt, carries off souls in the sequence of their deaths—so that even if we were to die moments apart, we would never be able to reach one another?

Staring through the banisters at the top of the attic stairs, my legs tucked under me like a child, I sort papers in solitary confinement. The shock of hearing the bars slam shut at first distracts me from the dimensions of my cell, or the duration of my term. I notice only darkness all around me. Taking fearful, mincing steps to avoid crashing into a wall, I can detect no boundaries. Lengthening my stride, I break into a run. In every direction I dash to the point of exhaustion—and still there is no end to the emptiness. I'm terrified of being parted from Jean-Paul. Only the ground on which I stand provides a point of reference, until suddenly it drops from under me! I am suspended in black space—alone.

·

Evanston. September, 1973

It is as if we have been in a blind fog, adrift in a tiny life boat. Now Jean-Paul finds the conviction that he can direct us to shore—but we must learn to row as one. We keep the port of Unity in mind. There each of us will find hope in our belief in one another.

In fact, we undertake this goal like any other joint endeavor—with scratch paper and pens. Pulling up two chairs to any horizontal surface, we make of it a partners' desk, where we devise our new philosophy of oneness through sketches and poetry, exposition, diagrams. We co-author The Blue Book, as if writing the most rigorous exam.

Conceiving a vision, Jean-Paul tries to quell our terrors by forging a new religion for us in the flames of love and art. It feels dangerous to me. The more fugitive the life that he envisions for us, the more aware I am that there is nothing, except him, tying me to this world.

Sensing I yearn for the comfort of normalcy, he tries to curb his grandiosity. But something he senses in the darkness drives him to push the boundaries of the possible as hard as he can. He rows faster than ever.

Finally, it is I who stops his hand midstroke—with one passionate sentence. Words I thought could never pass my lips, form in my solar plexus, sound themselves in the verboten "what if" struggling from my throat. "What if . . . what if . . . trying to be one with you . . . is making me feel I have NO SOUL OF MY OWN?"

It is stunning. And it is out. My jaw slackens. Have I just ravaged all we've been striving for? Jean-Paul looks as if he's been slapped. But there can be no retraction.

The Blue Book is shut. We withdraw our hands from it as if they have been burned. No, worse than that—as if in striving for oneness, we have burned each other's hands—mine, in the fire of Jean-Paul's visions—his, on the dry ice of my objection.

Evanston. October, 1973

Stray snowflakes pirouette before the windshield. For the first time in weeks, I untether my thoughts. Snow falls . . . hope rises. Snow falls . . . hope rises while I set a daydream spinning . . . a romantic reverie about our agent, a man with children, who is nearly old enough to be my father.

Should I confess my fantasy to Jean-Paul? Ridiculous! Nothing will ever come of it!

Then, instantly, a dreadful question strikes—like a thought but weightier than thought—like a shock—but still more stultifying. DID I JUST HIT SOME-THING—SOMEONE? My eyes dart to the rear-view mirror. Nothing in the reflection is amiss—but I can't dismiss the question. Again and again my sight is drawn backward.

I drive straight home, and when inside, lean hard against the front door to shut out the awful warring between my senses and my self. Only then does it return to me—that I have driven this internal road before.

II

Was it only this morning I painted with such passion that I could understand van Gogh's desire to devour the pigment from his palette? Immobilized, I stare at the mysterious triptych on my easel, longing to tell Jean-Paul what is happening inside me. But I am fighting for us both and losing; the brutal dismantling going on behind my face will not wait for me to speak.

Years have repealed themselves within hours, until there is no buffer between myself and the worst of my past symptoms. Invisibly, soundlessly within the shell of my skull my authority's slipped. Power's fractured. I've become the accuser and the accused.

Just hours ago, my brain functioned normally—if only I could find the passage back to try again.

Evanston. November, 1973

There is no longer a single meaning to the word "*I.*" The self splinters. In my internal tribunal, multifarious *I's* accuse. A single *I* defends. The multitude of self-accusing *I's* is eternally awake, tag-teaming my prosecution.

"Guilty feelings this profound don't spring full-blown from nowhere!" an *I* arraigns itself. "They must be prompted by something I've done in the past—or something I want fervently to do."

"Only an unthinkable crime," another *I* proposes, "could account for the white heat of my guilt!"

"What crime, then? Name it!"—the single *I* strains to call their bluff. But she unwittingly raises the stakes, causing horrific offenses to flash instantly to mind. Each accusation overrides its precedent. Newspaper headlines writhe to reshape themselves as I walk by: "HIT AND RUN," "ABDUCTION," "SLAYING."

I return home wrung out and weeping—aching undeservedly to be held. Jean-Paul strokes my hair, and tells me, "Shhh—they're only symbols. We can tackle symbols. They're our stock in trade."

II

We name the witnesses for my prosecution "the accusing voices"—as if they were apart from me. We fortify ourselves against my enemies. But one voice—mine, like all the others, yet somehow male and more malevolent to me—exhibits a labyrinthine personality. He promises to help me expose that portion of my soul that so betrays my true morality.

Jean-Paul says, "You're trapped inside your mind with a voice as trustworthy as Iago—'honest Iago,'" he adds sardonically. "How can you submit to a voice that pretends to protect what it means to destroy?"

But I can only reason in horror: since my own Jean-Paul has called this voice of mine "Iago," then I embody that sinister identity. And as an Iago, there may be many victims I'm plotting to destroy.

Evanston. January, 1974

My pulse quickens with the sensation that my own evil cannot be contained within the walls of my body. I have been unscrupulous to trust myself alone. I need to make my way across town to Jean-Paul. From now on I must be watched over.

I trudge down what I suppose is our brick path winding under a foot and a half of snow. The roads are impassable. *This is insane.*

No. In the house I was insane. In the cold air, I feel my brain clear. How serenely silent is the snowfall. But I sense an eeriness about its unearthly peace. If only I were to thrust my arms forward—could I part its mystery like a curtain?

Iago whispers, "Suppose the deceitful part of you commits her guilty acts, then she represses them. Afterward you would be unaware of missing even a step!"

"Swoosh, swoosh. Swoosh, swoosh." I listen for the rhythm of my walking. Surely I could detect a missing beat if I attend closely enough.

But my thoughts veer off. An arraigning *I* is at my throat—"There! I missed some steps!"

"Meaningless!" I defend myself. "My mind only wandered."

"But why do you feel so evil?" Iago counters coolly. "If I were you, I would want an answer to that simple question."

Snow buffets my face as the accusations against me grow deeper and thicker. Like the flicker of an archived film, my vision pulsates. I blink at my watch. How long this is taking! I cannot account for so much time passing. Have I strayed from my path to commit some awful crime?

"The snow!" whispers a voice. "The snow will have the answer!" I turn to check. As far behind me as I can see lies the line of my tracks. Proof of my innocence!

But the after-image printed on my mind's screen does not jibe with what I've seen. I whirl to check again, turn back, become uncertain, check again. A painful sob wells in my throat, but I shake the distorting tears from my eyes. I mustn't let self-pity interfere with vigilance.

Evanston. February, 1974

What anarchy when the mind suspects its agents! My eyes have sensed that they increase the incidence of hazard, turn all probability toward disaster, cause the inconceivable to be. Now they deflect their gaze, beg me to shut the world from their abuse. My feet repent the crush of walking, warn of their capacity to trample, even stepping cautiously. I fold my thumbs within closed fingers, making harmless instruments of hands; but still, they claim old memories of violence, want to be observed continuously.

When the mind suspects its agents, they forsake themselves, extend the allegations, learn to confess. The body aggregate contends its touch contaminates. The mind, in turn, defers till they whose testimony should be heard with measured judgment, seize instead, the power to convict.

Ravine Road, Fairfield. September, 1974

Mother's fingers wrap around mine as we walk. There are only these few moments for the two of us to talk, before I depart with Jean-Paul for a film festival. I model my face into what I suppose might pass for a light-hearted expression. "We'll send you a postcard from Lincolnshire," I assure her.

But I am thinking of the wax doll which Grandmother Christianna gave to her when they lived in Toronto. I remember it as if I myself were Mother . . . how Grandmother warned her this precious doll must be cared for with even more caution than the porcelain-headed ones. It mustn't be squeezed or dropped. Its delicate hands must not be pressed too long between warm palms. It must never be left in the sun.

So Mother kept her waxen baby from the outdoors, from patches of sunlight on the floor. She kept the doll from the frantic hands of the twins, and played with her at night, when the moon would not be too much for her.

But then one day, Mother's vigilance began to wane. She left her waxen child on the brick wall of the porch, where the sun had its way with her. She found her beloved's face deformed and malleable—tried to pinch it back in place—molded a monster—hid it guiltily beneath the swing.

Grandmother went to the porch for a breath of air after dinner. She seated herself, and as her foot swung to and fro, at last it located the creature. Christianna summoned her daughter to the screen door—Lisbet would never be trusted with a precious doll again. How my heart aches for my little mother.

Suddenly, she takes my chin in her hand and turns my face toward her. She is the mother I most remember—the one who tried to encompass me in her protective sphere, the one who managed her fears by granting me the legacy of all her precautions, the one who taught me that to arrive at certainty I need only check and recheck, the one who was never sure—the one who ached for a mother.

She wants to search my soul, but I can't bear her eyes which might carry me back and back. She is insistent. Then for a terrifying instant she catches my soul in her glance and finds disfigurement. My heart plunges. This is the moment before Mother will blind herself to me again, before the screen insinuates itself between us—the one before she will begin to whistle those familiar hollow notes, like a little girl who, not knowing what to feel, cannot find a melody.

We turn and walk home, the sun braising my shoulders while Mother whistles in the dark.

London, England. October, 1974

Like Janus, god and guardian of gateways, I have two faces—one turned toward the past, the other toward the future. The first inspects memory. The second investigates desire.

Glancing at Jean-Paul asleep on our hotel bed, I complete an entry in our travel journal, making, as is my rule, no mention of my illness. It was he who suggested this vacation as an antidote to my symptoms. But they have only wormed their way deeper underground.

In this hidden search for my crime, I dig like a painstaking archaeologist through the strata of memory, unearthing transgressions day upon day. I sort and label furtive conversations, covert rages, primal cravings, guilty horrors—all dug up in the most taunting sequences.

Iago is faster with his pick than I, and stays invisibly ahead so he can toy with the mementos. As soon as I am certain every relic of an alleged incident has been unearthed, he stands back to revel in my white-knuckled arm wrestling against an accusing *I*. Iago knows that he conceals behind his back the only missing piece of memory which could prove my innocence.

He waits until my brain throbs, heart pounds—until my clenched hand is pressed nearly to the ground in forced confession—before he tosses the precious token in the air. I catch it against my breast and hate him, knowing he'll return to torment me again tomorrow. Has he ever relinquished a trophy without higher stakes in mind?

Still, in the moment of my acquittal, relief pours—not as a metaphor, but in a palpable sensation—just beneath my skull. I feel a cold liquid flow in icy rivulets over the top of my brain. Reality clears, releasing me to face another day, to unearth another layer.

I gaze at Jean-Paul sleeping so soundly. Since I can't live with the oneness we longed for, I've begun to live for this chill I crave.

II

The mind cannot review its own performance—will not say if that was memory which moved upon its stage, or merely rear-projected fear. For the disparity in the brain is only chemical, between a past atrocity and present fear cast backward.

But that disparity directs a crucial spectacle: the contest of evidence to prove my soul's corruption, or my mind's mismanagement.

Lincolnshire, England. November, 1974

We stand in a little church yard in Lincolnshire, directed here by an old man in the newspaper office, who remembers Grandfather after all these years. Dry leaves swirl into eddies at our feet as we peer down at a worn head stone:

ANNA PEMBERTY, 1902-1904

I'd almost forgotten this mysterious child with one name the same as mine, the other the same as Mother's. This must be the baby whose picture still appears on Mother's dresser. How odd. She never speaks of her.

A voice makes a stab in the dark—testing me to see if I will accept this child as one of my many victims. And I'm pleased, for once, to turn the tables on my accuser. How could I have harmed someone who died before I was born?

Chicago. Halloween Eve, 1975

Snowflakes are herded over the expressway by a ferocious wind, so that Jean-Paul struggles to keep our Volkswagen on the road. But the bitter cold is no match for the freeze between us as we recall our public exposure. How I had begged Jean-Paul to speak without me at our screening. But he has wearied of carrying our compounded weight.

Before the crowd, my voice quavered while I fought back tears, so that I had to look beseechingly to him to complete my every answer. I contributed nothing to the evening except the eerie impression that the duo, whom the audience had come to meet, shared only one functioning mind. Which of us feels more mortified?

Quietly losing one aspect at a time of our once vibrant marriage, we have never tallied our losses the way we do tonight in frigid silence. Jean-Paul fights the wind. And at each startling sound the wind provokes, I fight the urge to beg him to retrace our route . . . in case we've struck something—someone.

Old newspapers, long forgotten by the roadside, are swept up and animated, flitting across our windshield—counterfeit ghosts.

Evanston. Halloween, 1975

Absorbed in our annual ritual, our dearest friend delivers the first strike of his knife into the would-be jack-o-lantern with childlike gusto. But as I turn to see the blade pierce the pumpkin's shell, it is all I can do not to grab his arm, beg him to go no further. Am I witnessing a kind of rape, castration, murder? I try to shake the deception from my head—but there remains the urgent conviction that I have to save . . . to save *what*? To save a *baby's* life . . . a baby *imprisoned* in the pumpkin shell. I turn away, attempt to laugh. "At last, I've hit bathos!"

But however mad, the delusion quivers with its own import. Is the awful secret I have been trying for two years to unearth, at last revealing itself in a kind of code? Do I now know who my own victim was—or will be? Someone small and helpless . . . a . . . I can hardly say the word, even to myself . . . a . . . *baby*.

"How horrible for you," whispers Iago empathetically. "Sometime, somewhere you must have injured—perhaps murdered—a baby, so viciously that you can't recall it!"

Inside my skull, my brain reels; then—an implosion of self-hatred. I picture raising a gun to my temple. Nothing could be as satisfying as pulling the trigger. Nothing. It is cruel of Jean-Paul to try to keep me here.

Maybe I don't need a gun. I almost feel as if I could, without a tell-tale sound, focus my loathing with such intensity at my own brain that I could extinguish myself from the inside, with no one being aware.

Evanston. November, 1975

In that momentary piercing of the pumpkin's shell, whatever membrane I'd maintained between the world within and the world without—between thought and action—was finally breached. And the chaos I'd fought so hard to contain burst out, as I knew in my darkest dreams one day it would.

Now my brain teems in a mixed-media frenzy. If I borrow a smear of crimson from a passing car, I can turn a puddle to a pool of blood. I warp sound waves as they near so that, by the time they reach my ear, babies wail—where no babies are. From their burial places beneath stone paths, within plaster ceilings, my tiny victims moan for mercy, so that I must beg Jean-Paul to be all my senses.

He comprehends as well as I that no amount of checking could convince me of my innocence. Yet this is how he ransoms for me one more instant, one more hour, before I will surrender to the chorus of accusing voices.

Now that Iago's found in me the tenderest spot to twist his knife, I know decidedly that this will be the final arena. The old array of symptoms, so intolerable since the onset of my illness, pales next to the immediacy, the utter urgency of these.

II

Within each human corridor, there are just two escapes. The way of suicide is manifest—its latch undone. The second door's the one that destiny has hung. Most disregard the first escape, and stay to be aligned with fate.

No hinge denotes, no seam forecasts, no latch betrays the second door. If it is hidden in a wall, some day by chance I'll see it open mincingly— allowing cognizance and agony. If it is buried in the floor, it will collapse—haphazardly. Why honor destiny?

Oh, Jean-Paul, let me keep the door of suicide ajar. For when it's shut by someone else's hand— however silently—I hear it slam.

III

My illness has come between us like a curtain slowly drawn. How bland the word sounds for something standing as our last remaining hope—therapy. With my eyes tightly closed during the endless drive to my first appointment, I can picture the last leaves of autumn, brown and withered, curling inward, a few of them still clinging to the trees. Let go, let go! Why do I still hang on at all?

Jean-Paul is the single reason—more my brother now, somehow, than husband. I risk a glance in his direction. "Promise you won't kill yourself," he whispers—his voice breaking. "How could I bear to stay alive, if you died for crimes that never were?"

He looks like a vulnerable child. Nodding in hesitant assent, I close my eyes again. The miles roll under us, our fingers stretching to intertwine on the seat between us, as we ride in silent suspension between despair and longing—afraid to hope, afraid not to hope.

Part Three
(1978)

Ravine Road, Fairfield. July, 1978

When she lay dead in her glass coffin, was her brain alive? Snow White, I mean. Did she dream? Can you dream if you know you have no future? Or only remember, like me? Could she feel? Were her feelings alive, or paralyzed like mine?

Before they gave me up and laid me out like this, many had tried to revive me. The first therapist thought he could startle me from my enchantment. But I only jumped at the deliberate slam of his unabridged dictionary on the desk behind me.

The second thought the cure was chemical. So I had to ratchet up my vigilance—since all my sentinels got drunk.

The third thought he could waken me with love.

I can see his hand rubbing the leather arm of his chair, passionately, while he caressed me with his eyes. So I became more culpable for all the thoughts he stirred. He never understood how I could leave him.

The fourth tried to restore me with intellect alone. And when my feelings finally rose in protest, she shamed me for their childishness—and so, they closed.

I lie all day in my glass coffin, atop the bed I slept in as a child, while my pulsing brain strains in my rigid body to think its way out of the impossible bind. If, as Iago calculates, my victims by now number more than Hitler's, then nothing short of suicide is justified.

And yet, the single thing I know with certainty is that unless I stay alive—at least enough to blink— Jean-Paul will die.

II

Mother approaches my bedroom. Through the glass casing of my casket I watch the truth descend like a zeppelin. It's always been there, hovering, looming in my sky—casting its gigantic shadow over me.

More enormous than I can conceive of, yet lighter than air—it weighs no more than a few words. Mother hurries down the ladder from the gondola, her face dark in its shadow.

She can't look at me without blaming herself. She must deliver her declaration to me in the nick of time, before the airship explodes into a fire storm behind her—and so she cries out: "I'm not going to let you do this to me any longer, Anna. I've been afraid of you—all your life!"

"You've been afraid of me . . . all my life?" I repeat in horror.

"All—your—life!"

In Flight from New York to Chicago. July, 1978

Mother is so relieved to see me go, she can't let me go. I'm the last passenger to board. But in the instant

the plane's steel door seals closed, protecting my per-
ishable mother from me, I am reborn. Born in a
rage—the child within me screaming back at
Mother's words: "All my life I've been feared? All my
life? Where is the justice in this?"

For the first time since the onset of my illness I
can nearly touch compassion for myself. If not quite
this—for the frantic child inside me. I am heading
home to Jean-Paul, who, no longer my husband, is
still the truest family I have ever known.

En route, I bargain with Iago on my own. I can't
assert my innocence without a backlash of symptoms.
Yet, I can say this to him for the first time: "I am a
human being. You can't deny me this. And if I've been
corrupted—surely I wasn't born corrupt. No one could
deny I've tried to root out my own evil. I've tried. I've
tried. Doesn't that make even the least human being
worth saving?" It is the best I can do, but it's no meager
benchmark. Iago, for the moment, is mute.

Knowing she's safe on the ground while I'm in

the sky, I allow myself the privilege of wrath toward a mother who could fear her tiny child. And simultaneously, I've never felt more grateful to her. For she's given me the gift no one but she could deliver to me: a testimonial, at last, to my most painful and primitive perceptions.

Chicago. July, 1978

If there were another cure, how gladly I would grasp it. But therapy remains the only avenue to health. Outside the waiting room before I meet Dr. Murray, Jean-Paul keeps me company, his strong hands gripping my shoulders.

I feel queasy as we stare down at the street, so many floors, so many stories below. The kind of stories we're both recalling all have sad endings. Unless, of course, we try to read them as merely setbacks in our unfinished tale.

We view these blocks along Michigan Avenue the way we would a blueprint of our recent lives. Inserting mental map pins, we mark with quips and comments the loci of our turning points.

There is the coffee shop in which our marriage ended. Now we can't even remember which of us proposed it—jesting in a fit of black humor that to overthrow our union might be just the last ditch act of complicity which could save our sinking ship. Looking into one another's eyes that night, how we enjoyed the fact that we could still laugh at such a joke together—until it dawned on both of us, in one dreadful engagement of our sights, that everything pointed to our divorce.

There is the lawyer's office. There is the building of Jean-Paul's therapist. Mine are scattered, yet still in view—the insertion of each pin causing a pain in my solar plexus.

And I wonder, when I look back at this appointment years from now, will its map tack mark a turn for the better—or one more stab to the heart?

II

Jean-Paul asks me to describe her. But I find I can't. After my appointment, I don't know the color of Dr. Murray's hair or eyes. I had been told ahead of time that she was very tall, but you couldn't prove that by me. Our eyes seemed to meet on a level. I cling to a single impression—that I've been permanently struck by an extraordinary match of form and content in her loveliness.

And so I say to Jean-Paul, "Remember the 'Seeker of Horses'?" At my rhetorical question, he launches into a Taoist tale committed to our common memory, "... *displeased, the Duke addressed Pei Lu: 'That friend of yours, Chiu Fang Yin, whom I sent to look for a horse, has made a farce of it. He sent word he had chosen a yellow mare—which turned out to be a jet black stallion. What, I ask, can he know about horses when he cannot even discern a creature's color or sex!?'*"

"Pei Lu sighed serenely," I add. *"'What Yin keeps in mind is the essence. Focused on the inward, he loses sight of the superficial.'"*

Jean-Paul races to the conclusion. *"When the horse arrived, it proved to be a superb animal, indeed."*

"You've proven to be a superb find," I assure Jean-Paul, "and so, I think, will Katherine Murray. Shall I remind you," I add with unaccustomed hope and self-satisfaction, "that I didn't know your eyes were blue until after we were married?"

Evanston. October, 1978

I flinch, catching sight of myself in the mirror after my shower. I'm all ribs, clavicle, cheek bones. When I mount the scale to verify my impression, 89 stares back at me. For the first time, I think I've begun to look—just slightly—like a survivor of a concentration camp. Nevertheless, I've begun to think I look like a survivor.

It's possible my eyes have never burned this brightly. I simply cannot eat. And I don't care that I can't eat. Tending my body is irrelevant to the obsession of mending my mind. I've nearly touched the other shore—nearly reached Katherine's side.

It's only because she gazes steadfastly, both at and through my illness, to find our common human roots, that I've been able to make my way to her. It's only because of what could never be said with words, that her words stand as stones, rocks, boulders across raging rapids, the waters beneath me still roiling with accusing voices.

On each rock I've teetered, balanced, slipped, regained my footing before lunging for the next. The swirling logic of Iago works away—wears away at her statements. Yet I'm unafraid that in a lifetime there could be enough erosion to destroy these stones under my feet.

Suddenly weak, I wrap my robe around myself and curl up on my bed until I have to leave for my appointment. Ignoring my hunger, I crave only memories of the trail of rocks by which I've nearly forded my illness.

II

I revisit my first appointment. Unable to face—yet one more time—my clinical history, I've handed a sheaf of papers to Dr. Murray on which I've typed an original fairy tale.

She receives the unfolded leaves with as much grateful expectancy as if I've given her a plant in full bud. Subtle expressions shimmer across her face as the story blooms beneath her eyes. Then, easily plucking the emblematic meaning from the tale, she offers it back to me, braided into a garland of my essential history.

"You already know so much about yourself," she says. "You're just not ready to say it outright yet—I think the idiom we'll share will be the language of symbols."

III

Weeks have passed. As I slip into the chair across from her, my mouth is sand, my stomach tight as a clam shell. I've reviewed what I want to convey to her. Now I say it all outright: that I know all my relationships with men have been futile attempts to exonerate myself from my guilt toward my mother; that I know the fervent notions of oneness on which I've built my life will have to topple further; that I know I've been my mother's mother and she my wounded child; that I know my symptoms are merely symbols of that reversal.

Exhausted, I want to add, "If it is truth that makes us free, then why do all my insights count for nothing? Why does Iago still have a strangle hold on me?" But I can only whisper through parched lips, "Please . . . could I have a glass of water?"

A wave of empathy ripples across Dr. Murray's face. She rises with instinctive grace and leaves the room without a word. Returning, she passes the tall, full tumbler to me. Then reading the appreciation in my eyes, she says, "This is more than a glass of water to you, isn't it? Tell me what it is."

Tears stream down my cheeks. "It's what I've needed—you're what I've needed to swallow the bitter pills of what I know. It's all been intellectual till now . . . until I found you."

"Drink up, then," she urges, smiling from her eyes.

IV

Inside my head, Katherine's voice has begun to defend me against my accusers. But I'm afraid—should my illness fade from sight too quickly—that I'll be denied her witness to its power and mystery.

"You don't have to become overwhelmed with symptoms ever again," she assures me. "We need only a tincture of them to study how they work."

With that, my symptoms begin to fall away from their cores like overripe and tainted fruit, leaving only vestiges of their flesh still clinging to the primal seeds. As we roll up our sleeves to examine the remains of my illness, Katherine lets them stain her hands just enough to apprehend their essence, permanently.

"When you feel disloyal—or critical—whenever your feelings rise from a sense of your own identity, you feel dangerous, Anna."

I take this seed from Katherine's hand, ". . . so I accuse myself of committing a crime, in order to arrest my sense of self."

"The accusations of the voices," she adds, "are alarms sounding, lights flashing. They indicate feelings you were taught to fear."

I peer more closely at the remains, investigate the seed's adhesions. "To be separate was to abandon Mother. I was taught to say 'we,' not 'I'; learned to say 'ours,' not 'mine.'" I rub my fingertips over the rugged pit, its convolutions rigid as a hardened brain, until the pain recalls to me that "criminal" was the word which mother paired with "selfishness."

V

I'm intrigued but uncomprehending, as Katherine snatches at an ephemeral insight. "This evening, I have the strongest sense," she says, "that your tormenting voices come directly out of your earliest childhood, Anna."

The notion flickers and fades and relumes itself like a lightning bug at dusk.

"I can't quite capture it, yet," she explains. "I can only say that, although I think you recognized them all, it would have been too dangerous for you to point a finger at your mother's irrational fear of you; or later, at Mark's sadistic use of you; or at yours and Jean-Paul's folie à deux. It would have been 'disloyal.' You would have felt you were abandoning them."

A light is lambent in her eyes.

"Ever since your childhood, you could only signal your distress by pantomiming the madness all around you—in the simple hope that someday, someone would decipher the code!"

How I want Katherine's insight never to fade. But I can only nod at her—still miming what feels too treacherous to confirm with words.

VI

Now that I've begun to see around my illness, shame rasps and grates against the edge of victory. "I've put so many people through so much," I say. "But no one's endured more pain for me than Jean-Paul."

"You're right, of course," she says. "And yet, the truth cuts both ways. You had to have this illness, Anna, to save yours and Jean-Paul's lives. Somewhere deep inside, you knew that both of you were doomed by your oneness."

"We need such different futures, just to survive," I say.

"But to leave your marriage by any other means than self-destruction would have seemed to you a betrayal. So, you made an object lesson of yourself by which you hoped that—one day—Jean-Paul, too, would see what had to be."

Katherine's light glints from both edges of the blade. But each revelation blinds me only briefly to those which have preceded it. I've traveled far beyond needing a single answer to the meaning of my illness. How often I say to myself these days, "and this, too, is true . . . and this, too . . . and this, too."

VII

I tear myself from the trail of stones, rocks, boulders by which I've nearly reached the other shore. Still famished, and still sickened by the thought of food, I pull myself up slowly from my bed to dress for my appointment.

Aboard the Chicago and Northwestern train into the city, it's still not easy to hold the voices at bay. The sensory input from the crowds is still rife with raw material for my delusions. But today I can almost lose myself under the spell of the François

Truffaut film I saw last night.

The Wild Child is the true story of a feral boy captured in the forest, where he has survived, like an animal, his own abandonment. How my heart goes out to him—trapped inside his mind, with no words to define or defend himself against the speculation of the curious, as to whether he is more idiot or beast. I don't know why I feel such kinship with his muteness. But I see his teacher in the same light as Katherine, as he uncloaks the child's humanity.

By the time I'm seated across from her, I'm feeling sorry for my parents. "I think I was a difficult and willful child," I say.

"I think you simply saw too much. Your perceptions have always threatened someone," Katherine says. "No one has known what to do with a little creature like you. But now, you're my wild child."

She looks into my eyes and, seeing I'm suddenly poised and quivering to make that last immeasurable leap to her, she stretches out her hand across the water. "Anna," she declares emphatically, "now you belong to *me*." And with the firm tug of her words, she pulls me to the banks of sanity.

Part Four
(1986-1994)

Evanston. August, 1986

I wake abruptly to the blackness of our bedroom, my face contorting into a soundless scream—remembering. No—not quite remembering. I waken *knowing* at once and at last what has been so long a mystery. I waken naming my original crime. The utter irony of its pettiness and its profundity stuns me. Hasn't it been in plain view all this time?

Struck by such lightning, I am a tree felled silently in a forest. Was there no sound because the only would-be hearers sleep so deeply next to me? My little son's damp head rests peacefully against a branch, my husband's fingers tangle in the leaves at my crown.

My body being encased in wood, I can't feel myself breathe—but I can prove I'm alive, internally.

From the corners of my eyes my life spills out of me, streams down my temples, saturates the leaves on my pillow.

Truth may be light and lightning, but I'm not like Daphne, chaste and terrified by the god of light! Why was I transformed into this laurel tree? After all these years pursuing truth, is it now pursuing me?

• • •

I resist the urge to jostle Cam awake and whisper to him what I know. No. I can wait the passing of this night. Deep, luxuriant, and delineated as the lining of a womb, how different is the darkness contained within our room from those boundless nights of my own making.

I am, at last, my own North Star—one star in a constellation with Cameron and Julian, Katherine and Jean-Paul—my burning lights. Held in place by their gravity, I use their pull to steady me for what I perceive advancing from darkest memory as a siege of sorrow.

Is this what I've craved since Julian's birth? In the blackness, his tiny hand is slung across my waist in ownership. Capacious spirit, full of love and fury—two and a half—my own wild child: will bitter memory be the antidote to insure I won't, in my apparent wellness, be an unwitting carrier of symptoms to you? I can't set us on a course charted upon unknown stars, incalculable light-years removed. Am I finally ready to do for you, what I've been unable to do for myself: to trace my illness back along its route to find its roots?

• • •

Throughout the night, still petrified, I temper my anticipation and dread by fixing my gaze on the lights of Julian and Cameron, Katherine and Jean-Paul. Cam turns in his sleep, his hand brushing my thigh, and I fantasize his dream's inspired by our love-making last evening, before Julian found his way into our bed.

Gentle maverick, Cameron—how finely we're counterpoised. Out of your faith in life, you've made a garret for me where I work and grow in my own way. For this and for accepting, even loving, Jean-Paul as my brother, thankful tears stream onto my pillow.

And dear Jean-Paul, with clear-eyed looks, at last we can disclose to one another every facet of our selves we had resented sacrificing to our oneness.

Oneness . . . oneness . . . isn't it a poem which we commit to heart and mind from earliest days? We hear it murmured at our mother's breasts and then, bereft of those, we're left to copy down its endless verses, while we long for its second coming in a grown-up guise.

Whether the poem is sung or spoken, choreographed or mimed, it teaches each of us that blending two souls into one is the highest goal of love. But you and I, Jean-Paul, lived the poem of oneness all too earnestly. Years ago, what pain we might have spared each other, had we known—to save our own and one another's souls—we only had to burn a poem.

Ah, but Jean-Paul . . . what a poem!

My heart, so full of contrast between the present and the past, reaches out for Katherine. No longer needed as my savior, she's become my companion of the mind, the one best suited to help me sift and sort my life. I almost laugh, recalling our awful war when she was a new mother and I was a new wife. She insisted I extricate myself from my continued closeness with Jean-Paul in order to protect my marriage. How I taught her the meaning of "fierce loyalty"! By now, it seems that she and I are stronger for that breach—as if it marked my birth.

I draw lines between and among the stars in our constellation. Every line is a guy-wire holding me.

• • •

Fragments of memory begin to float toward me from every era of my life. I want the ones that ache most—the ones I feel in my body—the ones from when I was very young—the ones I've never been able to remember, until now.

And yet I'm drawn back to Fairfield, after my

first illness had forced me to surrender Barnard. As I lay on my bed in the evening, how I used to listen to my father's chisel, as he patiently chipped away at the layers of paint on a primitive pine armoire from Quebec.

He worked methodically through the layers of pigment until he reached the one he wanted—teal blue. It would be scarred by his own chisel; it would be somewhat tinged by what had come after; it would reveal glimpses of what had come before; but teal blue was the gold he mined.

It would take him all that winter, as every night he mounted the stairs to his studio where he tapped and chipped, while I listened. I only hope his patient endurance became ingrained in me, so I can uncover the layer of memory I pine for.

I remember Father as I last saw him in the hospital. After showing us a sketch of the cradle he had hoped to build for his expected grandchild, he bequeathed his woodworking tools to Cam that night. But he gave his eyes to me. Our last communion of silent looks was interrupted by a strident nurse, who must have found it too weighty. In the months after his death, how I wove a cocoon of privacy around my feelings for Father.

Suddenly, I don't want the pain of recalling any further. But Julian's soft breath so near my ear reminds me—there is a reason for this backward peeling. Through a crack in the blinds I watch and wait patiently, as the black sky fades to Prussian blue and then to teal, before the dawning.

Chicago. August, 1986

At finding hidden aquifers of memory, our conscious minds are no more reliable than would-be water diviners. The source, itself, will never rise again. Yet, the ground waters of experience, secreted in spaces around gravel-hurts and grains of time—pressed hard enough through layers of rigid rock, will one

day spring in artesian tears. When the well-springs
are ready, they do not need to be divined . . . .

∙ ∙ ∙

I had never been held like this before, so far from
my Mama's body. I kept my confusion and terror
encased behind carved lips. In my baby-sitter's house,
I had ignited a firestorm! Then, I had sizzled the
inside of the car with lightning!

Stunned by my own powers, I was a rigid doll on
Mama's lap all the long drive home. I needed to hide my
head on her breast; instead she held me, face to the
windshield. I couldn't see my mother's eyes, but I could
glimpse the cruelty in Papa's every time they flashed to
the rear view mirror. What did he see in that glass?
Could it reveal what I'd done to damage all three of us—
Mama and Papa and me? I kept my eyes fixed on it.

∙ ∙ ∙

From Katherine's couch, I am suddenly drawn
back to the first symptom of my illness: *a dreadful question strikes—like a thought but weightier than thought—*

*like a shock—but still more stultifying: DID I JUST HIT
SOMETHING—SOMEONE? My eyes dart to the
rear-view mirror. Nothing in the reflection is amiss—but I
can't dismiss the question.*

"I could never divine what I had done to cause
my guilt," I say to Katherine, "until the other night,
when I awoke naming my first crime. Countless
times, the tale has been recounted to me in Mother's
quavering voice . . . 'You transferred your loyalty in
two short weeks.' And yet, as only one legend of a
thousand-and-one hurts, I never recognized that the
crime I sought so fervently was simply this: I ran, tod-
dling, to the wrong arms—and so became a traitor in
my mother's eyes."

Chicago. January, 1987

I float supine on the surface of a sea of tears, until
its current swallows me. The patch of sunlight
flashing on the cellophane skin of the sea grows

dim above me, fading to black.

At the top of the stairs on Gray Street, I find a baby doll in my own lap. But I can remember no further. The precious moments of my appointment slip by wordlessly.

Sinking deeper in these waters than I've ever been before, I feel a gentle jarring at my back. Could I have touched bottom? A focused beam lights something of substance swirling down to me. I reach out for a conch, long vacated by the creature it once housed. It is a shell, like knowledge, representative and true in form, but empty of feeling.

I turn its paradox in my hand: immersed in this sea of tears, the shell is utterly dry . . . as hollow as my own voice. "I think I threw the doll," I say dispassionately.

Dry sand, slipping through the cinched glass of time, begins to pour in multiples of its appointed speed. And though she sits behind me, I feel a growing tension in Katherine.

Becoming my childhood-self, I turn my face to the wall as my hands gesture mechanically—the rigid fingers of my one hand tap, tap, tapping rhythmically against the outstretched tips of my other fingers—

Katherine shatters my eternity. "This feels wrong to me—all this eerie stillness! It's so completely out of the blue! Why today? It feels . . . you feel *autistic* to me, Anna!"

Memory swirls into the arid shell, filling it with feeling. "I hated the doll! It was a baby. I didn't need to be a baby anymore and play with dolls. I wanted to get rid of it—just like the baby in me. I threw it against the railing!"

Do I now know who my own victim was? Someone small and helpless . . . a . . . . I can hardly say the word, even to myself . . . a . . . baby.

"Those wounded babies I saw night and day," I gasp, "looked just like that doll!"

Katherine's skirt rustles as she moves closer in her chair to me. My hands take on a desperation of their own, wringing themselves as if they weren't my hands at all.

Between my words a mournful sound—the forgotten note of my world on Gray Street—resonates from the top of my throat, "Uhnnn, Uhnnnn . . . . I rushed to where the doll landed. Uhnnnnn . . . . I picked it up and cradled it. I ached to undo what I had done. The doll was not the-baby-in-myself any longer."

"Anna . . . you'll have to be my little mother now . . . ."

"The doll is . . . Mother now."

"Yes!" says Katherine.

I am my childhood-self turning the doll over and over in my lap, checking—rechecking its damage—trying to take care of it. Now I stare at the banisters, making them into prison bars for myself.

I have no word for it but 'jail.'

Staring through the banisters at the top of the attic stairs, my legs tucked under me like a child, I sort papers in solitary confinement. The shock of hearing the bars slam shut at first distracts me from the dimensions of my cell, or the duration of my term. I only notice the darkness all around me.

During the evening train ride home, reflections of my childhood-self superimpose themselves over the smoky windows. I return again and again to the top of the stairs, cradling my toy gun. I aim it at my temple. Nothing is as satisfying as pulling the trigger. Click!

Nothing. It is cruel of Jean-Paul to try to keep me here. Maybe I don't need a gun . . . . I almost feel as if I could, without a tell-tale sound, focus my loathing with such intensity at my own brain that I could extinguish myself from the inside, with no one being aware.

Ravine Road, Fairfield. February, 1987

Mother's percussive coughing nicks at the edges of my sleep, chips at my consciousness, until I give up my fold in Cam's and Julian's blanketed nest, for a nearby chaise overlooking her ravine.

Ricocheting from one impenetrable surface to another, Mother's cough erupted earlier at the granite table, as I recorded her siblings' names and birth dates for Julian's ancestral tree. About the firstborn daughter I asked, "Did Grandmother often speak of Anna?"

"ALL THE TIME!" The words surged past Mother's lips like prisoners through an unexpected gash in a barbed wire fence.

"It must have been hard on you," I whispered.

But the cruel hand of her warden snatched back the liberated words, "I didn't mean what I said—"

II

From Mother's chaise, I stare down at the naked spot-lit oaks in her ravine.

Listening through her chronic coughing for Julian's steady breath, I am three women on this midnight—Christianna, and Lisbet and I—roots, trunk and branches of a single tree. Secret and systemic, the nature of our shared disease is becoming evident to me: how many decades have our defective fruits been plucked under cover of night, so the eyes of the world would not find them? A voice of solitude wells up from our roots . . . .

How many years, Love, has this house been stamped with my infection? I'm not referring to germs, for once, nor my influenza, nor the pneumonia to which it's turned.

I'm speaking of my obsession, my contagious fearfulness since Anna died. I can detect its shadow—but too late, I think—darkest at Lisbet's window, yet discernible through every chink.

Our genealogy is stark and manifest in its branching, like a skeletal tree tonight, as I remember a therapist once asking, "Could you have had a sibling who died before you were born? Your symptoms fit that circumstance so undeniably." Why were my mother's symptoms handed down, instead, to me?

I take a hard look at our family tree, so outwardly exemplary that only its rings could tell the story of our years: droughts and floods of tears, fires of family loyalties, grafting of new affections, scars of their severance.

Yet more than to these, my eyes are drawn to the widest rings—to those hearty seasons of my middle childhood, when Lisbet's deepest love and creative spirit had seemed to overcome our roots' disease— then, nearer to the center of the tree, to what I know instinctively is the narrowest marrow of my early childhood.

My vantage point is highly moveable tonight. Peering into the ravine, I imagine myself a wanderer in a mystical forest—in which every tree is a family's story. The trees too near my path seem to speed behind me so that I can't hold them in my view. The ancient forms at a distance are so much easier to perceive. So many of these have been overturned—their desiccated roots aglow tonight in the moonlight, like sun-baked bones and antlers.

Is my family's story so patently different from most? In degree alone, I think. Isn't it only when we stumble over the tops of living roots—their soil eroded by pain and time—that we are reminded: half our lives are underground? These risen roots can lead our eye awhile, until they dive below, to veer we don't know where. And still, we have a sense of their direction.

In the cross-section of my family tree, I gaze again at the three attenuated rings which represent the years we lived on Gray Street. They bear such replication of those scars at the trunk's very heart—my precipitous illness at the age at which another Anna died, the three consecutive winters of my mother's pneumonia. How afraid she must have felt to die; how guilty to survive her mother's disease.

I begin, at last, to see that during the lonely hours, upon days, upon weeks of our shared confinements, our family history was reenacted. And as Mother relived, and I reacted, we imbued the house on Gray Street with quiet madness.

TIMELESS *Gray Street*

I reach a plump hand above my head to turn a knob of porcelain on the stairway door, and the centennial house on Gray Street opens magically for me. It must be moving day, for I am nearly knocked backward by the shock of a craggy mountain of wooden stairs daring me to my room.

One-foot, two-feet. One-foot, two-feet. Halfway, it is dizzying to look down, daunting to look up; and I begin to wail with my head on the next step. "Carry me?" I beg my mama, when she appears at the door.

Mama shakes her head. "You're not a baby any more!"

You stop to bleat your tears, start to scramble backward to me. I cannot let you, Lisbet. Every step for me is too painful to repeat. I have become the shepherdess charged with your deliverance beyond the age when Anna died.

II

When my mother lays cold towels on my blazing forehead . . .

Oh, why did I ever name her "Anna"?

. . . I gather up her fingers to keep her next to me. They are like red crayons in torn paper wrappers.

My hands assume your fervor on their own. I won't stop scouring until I find a tracery of your

blood in the cracks of my knuckles. There's noth-
ing I wouldn't do to save our child.

Dear God, could such a creature who, just twelve
days past, ruled a wild kingdom from my lap, be
vanquished at two-and-a-half?

III

I feel the pinch of my legs tucked under me as I
pitch forward and back, backward and forth, like a
rocking horse on the floor beside my mother's
couch. For the moment, I have released my hands
from where I keep them entrapped between the
floor and my shins.

Did you see these hands as spirit wings—to carry
me away? I'll never leave you, Mother. Don't be
afraid.

I am the child again who is merged with the form-
less shape of my ailing mother under the blankets . . .
and all her imaginings. I rub my numb fingertips over

the nubby surface of the carpet until they tingle—assuring me I am still here, where I need to be, at my station beside her couch.

When she is not coughing, Mama's body jerks at every sound, at every creak or squeak or buzz or hum that a house makes. "Is that you, Anna?"

But I cannot answer. On my tongue is an aborted word, and in my throat—a cry forever truncated. At my center gapes an emptiness as large as my mother, which hurts like hunger. "Uhhhnnn . . . uhnnnn . . . .

"Is that you humming?"

"Is that you, Dear, on the stairs? Is that you in the kitchen, Anna? Promise you won't get into the knives!"

On the borders of my vision flit my own quick and suspicious movements as I enter and leave myself to do what only Mama knows for sure, for I cannot catch myself.

IV

You swore me to secrecy. Now, I've become Cinderella. I'm sure my grief for you has been as great as hers for her mother. Why is there no magic hazel tree above your grave to flourish from my tears? Where is the small white bird to shower down upon me what I need from you?

Mama cries, "It's a shame you're having to be the little mother all day long, Anna . . . just like me."

As I rock myself in Mama's lap, her words sing-song in my ears, "All-day-long-all-day-long."

There is no border between my child and me. No boundary.

"Mustn't tell anyone I spoke to you like this . . . ." my mother begs me.

Words assemble inside my head, but my mouth will not shape them for me . . . "I promise. I promise."

"Mustn't tell anyone I talk to you this way. It would *kill* me if you did!"

Didn't Mama say the awful word again? Yes—if I ever let the secrets she is pouring into my ears escape through my lips, I will *kill* my mama, whom I love the best. Her voice seems to stream from the cuts which are her eyes. I feel my stomach tighten into a fist, ready to defend her against whatever hurts her, especially myself.

But what exactly is the secret for today? "Your father has threatened to leave us . . . ." The words and the sobbing intertwine like ropes of water strangling me. "But he loves you more than he does me, Anna, so you must help to keep him with us. You must be very grown up from now on—that's what Papa wants. You mustn't be a baby any more!" Mama puts me on the floor.

Even if I have to seal my mouth forever, I'll never let her secrets out. I won't let my mother die or Papa leave us.

I turn myself into a pumpkin shell, tipping back and forth—"Pe-der Pe-der Pum-kin E-der Hada Wif-un Coud-un Kee-per . . . ."

*In that momentary piercing of the pumpkin's shell,
whatever membrane I'd maintained between the
world within and the world without—between
thought and action—was finally breached. And the
chaos I'd fought so hard to contain burst out, as I
knew in my darkest dreams one day it would.*

". . . Pu-der In-na Pum-kin She-len Ther-e Kep-
per Ver-y Wel-un Pe-der Pe-der Pum-kin E-der Hada Wif-un Coud-un Kee-per."

V

From the inside of the pumpkin, where I keep my
mama well, I feel ice melting—flooding—over the
top of my shell.

*. . . a cold liquid flows in icy rivulets over the top
of my brain. Reality clears . . . .*

I am in the air, suspended in Papa's strong hands.
I begin to hear his voice, underwater . . . "What's the

matter with Anna? She's as stiff as a statue, and she won't look back at me!"

"Uhhnnnn . . . uhnnnn."

"She's all right," says Mama's voice over her shoulder from the couch. "She's only humming. She's been humming all afternoon."

"I tell you, that's not humming. She shouldn't be alone with you all day when you're so sick."

"All-day-long-all-day-long." The words sing-song in my head. Papa's hands felt warm when he lifted me. But he has set me on the floor again, and now my teeth begin to chatter.

When I've thawed, I totter on stilt legs to my father, and lay my cheek on one of his bony knees sticking out from the newspaper. He rubs my head in his two hands, and looks into my eyes. "Sugarpie, you had me scared," he says.

He snaps again at Mama's back under the blankets. "It's not good for her to be alone with you all day!"

Mama starts to cry. "Then why don't you stay home from work and care for her?" she says, trying to sit up.

Papa explodes at Mama.

No more White Knight.

I run to pat her hand. Papa growls at me, "The trouble with you, Anna, is you don't know who's on your side." And he slams out the front door.

He watches me rip along my core, both halves dropping at his feet.

I am lifted to my wounded mother's lap, and, making sure I have my baby-mama with me, I back deeper inside the pumpkin, so no one can peer at us through my jack-o-lantern eyes.

VI

In-side-out-side-in-side-out. Through the mullioned window I see that outside—where Papa's gone—it's snowing, snowing.

Glitter is sifted in front of a blackened sky. The snowfall softens the "whoosh" of traffic on Riverside Drive, muffles the shriek of subway brakes at 116th and Broadway, so it can whisper to me, privately.

I rub Mama's wet cheeks with my thumbs. "It isn't you who hurt me, it's your father," she tells me with her broken lips.

If my rage has poisoning power, let it be to fortify my child with the antigens of anger. Didn't Thetis dip her infant head first in the River of Death to steel him?

Mama hates Papa—he hurts her so.

Inside the pumpkin shell on her lap, I work to bob atop her coughing and sobbing, so the two of us don't drown. I turn my head to watch the snowflakes sliding down the window panes. Papa went outside. In-side-out-side-in-side-out-side.

Minutes slide. I watch the rivers ripple down the

inside of the windshield. What am I waiting for?
If only once I had seen a tear glimmer in your
eye, Father, then there might have been a con-
test. But Mother needs me. And you, it seems,
need no one.

Inside-outside. My tears will not stay down
where I can keep swallowing them back. Mama
notices, and then—behind her face—she does
something to hurt herself badly. After that, I turn
clear as water.

Once Anna's eyes drew mine like magnets. Now
they repel my gaze. I cannot look in them without
blaming myself.

Mama doesn't see me anymore. I climb down to
the floor. Rocking, rocking, I ride atop her galloping
coughing to rein it in and make it stop.

Each recurrent wave of her coughing engulfs us both.
Yet it recedes only to drag her farther out to sea.

Uhhnnnn, is Mama's dying? Uhhnnnn, has Papa

left us? Uhhhnnnn—did I let some secrets out?

Shhhhhhhhh . . . what's that soothing sound? The air rushing from the heat vent? No. It is the whispering of the conch my papa gave to me. It felt rough outside, and smooth inside. Its sound was white as snow and pink within—and pearl. "Listen to the ocean, Anna," Papa told me, as he lifted me in his arms and held the pretty shell to my ear.

Shhhhhhhhhhh . . . I listen so closely to its whispering, that the sound of the conch shell claims my soul.

I watch the snowflakes spiraling, spiraling against the night sky until—without leaving my mama—I find a way out through the sides of my skull.

More than a year must have passed, since that first snow last winter whitened—widened—the ravine between my senses and myself.

My rocking, rocking, is like a potter's furious pedaling, on the brink of the moment she will shape her own creation—on the brink of the moment her wheel flies on its own.

Snow falls . . . hope rises. Snow falls . . . hope rises while I set a daydream spinning . . .

Shhhhhhhhh . . . slowly, slowly, the lift of my wishes, which at first seemed evanescent, crests into no less than amaranthine hope. Ceaseless, seamless hope gathers in drifts of white feathers, crystal glitter, angel wings and snow . . . snow . . . snow . . . snow . . . .

If only I were to thrust my arms forward—could I part its mystery like a curtain?

Shhhhhhhhh . . . snow blankets every sound in feather down. Wordless, blank and safe . . . safe . . . safe. Every miniature flake is full of import in this saturated light.

The snowfall is all that is beautiful to me, and nearly all that matters. I turn into an angel of seren- ity. After Papa goes to bed tonight, I'll drift soundlessly on white wings down the mountain of stairs, and find him sleeping.

Papa will wake and look at me and, magically, know what to do to make peace with my mama. I won't even need to open my lips. I won't let the secrets or my mother out.

• • •

A flood of water is rising up, up against my second story window. "Papa—are we safe?!" My own voice inside my shell wakens me. My chest is a bellows filling and voiding with noiseless sobs. I sit up in bed. There is no water at the window, only twirling snow against a blackened sky.

I tuck my legs under me; and rocking, rocking, I set my hopes rising. I hear the guiding words in my head. "I-needa-go-down-stairs un-see-my papa-a-lone. I-needa-go-down-stairs un-see-my papa-a-lone."

In the dark, I am afraid to try my wings, and so I have to back down the mountain on bare feet. One-foot-two-feet.One-foot-two-feet. I-needa-go-down-stairs—one-foot-two-feet—un-see-my papa-a-lone. One-foot two-feet. I-needa-go-down-stairs—one-foot-two-feet—un-see-my papa-a-lone.

He is asleep, just as I imagined, but—so far from reach. I had forgotten Mama's bed comes first. My wings tingle at my shoulders as I quiver in the doorway. Angel of peace, I take a quiet step toward my father's bed. The floor creaks—and Mama's eyes startle wide—"What are you doing down here? Do you need me, Anna?"

I am an angel fallen from grace; for tonight I don't need Mama. It's Papa I need! My wings thump down the mountain behind me as I scuttle up the stairs.

VII

When the sun comes, my mother calls me down to her and steers me by the shoulders to the kitchen door. "These are children's footprints in the snow," she snaps. "Are any of them yours?" My nose is pressed against the glass. "Anna! Did you try to leave your mother in the night?"

A wail of horror breaks through the wall of my mouth. I back up further in the pumpkin as Mama spins it around. Why does she search my jack-o-lantern eyes for such an answer, when only she knows how I enter and leave my shell. I can never catch myself.

Now her angry eyes turn into frightened mirrors of mine. "Your boots will have the answer." Checking them, she satisfies herself. "You didn't go outside." But still my heart thunders.

Mama pulls me on her lap upon the couch and cries, "I was so afraid for you, Anna." And then her tears begin to fall.

If only, years ago, I could have thrown the sluice gates open . . . let my tears stream from every pore, cascade in rivulets down the bed-skirt to the floor, surge across a sodden rug, swell to the wainscoting, shatter the window panes, burst the doors, break our clandestine quarantine—

"I never forgot my perfect mother." Mama's voice seems to pour from her wounded eyes. "But if I died, Anna, you would soon forget me—the way you did in two short weeks."

What is Mama saying? Her face is breaking to pieces like Humpty Dumpty. "Don't you know you broke my heart when you ran from me?" she asks. I have no words to answer. But if running breaks my mother's heart, I won't run anymore.

> . . . *that I might have infected everyone with just a tincture of my caution . . . and thereby spared those I've loved most, the paralyzing dose.*

Once again on the carpet, I try to rein in my rocking horse's powers to do harm.

Shhhhhhhhh . . . . There is the magic sound again. From the floor, I stare through the wide window behind the hills of my mother's body. Outside, the evergreens are bent with spangling snow, and icicles are drip, drip, dripping from the eaves.

Shhhhhhhhhhh . . . . "Listen to the ocean, Anna," Papa told me. I hear the call of bells without sound—a silent carillon. This time I will listen to the song of the conch shell forever and ever. I will never leave this peaceful picture of the snow. It is all that is beautiful to me, and all that matters.

I am where I ought to be, beside my mother's couch. Hope soars. Ceaseless, seamless hope gathers again in drifts of white feathers, crystal glitter, angel wings and snow . . . snow . . . snow . . . snow.

Shhhhhhhhh . . . the rushing sound is changing: "Swoosh, swoosh. Swoosh, swoosh." If I attend closely enough I can hear the sound of my heart.

Then an impulse strikes—like a wordless thought, but more invincible than thought—like a shock, but more electrifying:

I *WANT* TO BE *OUTSIDE* IN THE SNOW. OUTSIDE—WHERE PAPA GOES. NOT IN-SIDE WITH MAMA, ALL-DAY-LONG-ALL-DAY-

LONG. I WANT TO SMASH THE GLASS—I WANT TO LEAVE-MY-MAMA!

Havoc smites my infidelity! "Swoosh-swoosh, swoosh-swoosh" is no longer the rush of my pulse, but the brush of my snow pants when I am walking. I think even Mama can't be sure—did I leave her in the night?—by the front door?—in my bare feet?

"The snow!" whispers a voice. "The snow will have the answer!"

An image of the untouched snow imprinted on my mind from the wide, wide window—alters. Black footprints—mine—burn into my picture, like charred spots from persistent flames held under white paper. The footprints spread and multiply, spoiling the purity of my snow. "Swoosh swoosh. Swoosh-swoosh." My leggings are brushing faster and faster. "Swoosh-swoosh-swoosh-swoosh—"

For one triumphant moment, I recover the ocean's summons from Papa's sea shell: "shhhhhh . . . ." For one triumphant moment I ride atop a cresting billow, until with a noiseless crash my white-capped wave rolls under. The pearl-white of my conch shell spirals into black.

Only the floor beside my mother's couch provides a frame of reference, until—

suddenly, it drops from under me! I am suspended in black space—alone.

Not a single muscle will obey my will. The lead weight of BLACKNESS presses against my chest.

• • •

I hear a baby cry. My jaw begins to tremble as I lie on Katherine's couch. I reach behind my head to touch her hand. As if exhumed from the loam of time, a voice I barely recognize as mine, gasps, "I want you to remember for me always. It was—death—worse than death. My pulsing brain . . . rigid body . . . I couldn't cry for help. I was gagged, bound, interred within a wall, or in the floor, underground—I could make no other sound than 'uhnnnnnnn.'

"This . . . this is what I've been running from all my life—what every symptom meant to save me from: terror, deep at the marrow, that any breach of loyalty might sentence me to an eternity—*buried alive.*"

Katherine releases a long-held breath—and her voice, too, seems altered. "I'll remember for you, Anna . . . all my life."

Chicago/Evanston. November, 1988

The meaning of the unexpected snow swirling outside of Katherine's window seems altogether changed from seasons past. No longer the seductive lure of madness twirling in hypnotic flakes, nor the piling up of accusations against me—I can make of this snowfall what I will.

As I fasten my coat I turn to Katherine, "Today the fear of another illness feels . . . behind me." She nods in agreement, confidently.

Downstairs, an icy gust of swirling discs greets me at the revolving door. What shall I make of them? The adding up of infinitesimal insights? A lift of hope, without an impending plunge to doom? They could be anything I extract from them.

With an appetite for celebration, I encounter two exultant family gifts in a museum shop on the way to the train station: a nesting doll for our collection, and a pop-up picture book.

The windows on the train, opaque with grime and nicotine, are as inscrutable today as when I was a novice to this journey. But the internal windows have achieved their own transparency.

On any given day, I might travel a lifetime to Gray Street—a door stands open at every station along the way. But I'm no longer afraid of these backward journeys, for I've learned to locate beauty only a single stop past horror.

Angling through the park, where the changing seasons have triggered in me so many anniversary memories, I let this overture of snow against the skeletal trees entice me to step again into my "dancing feet" as Father called them. I've taken the afternoon off and, unobserved, I dip and sway and twirl home circuitously.

Soon, Julian bangs in from junior kindergarten. "It's snowing—just like Christmas!" he announces jubilantly.

An impromptu holiday is just an easy sleight of mind for willing believers. Women and men of shortbread begin to leave their tracks in the flour, which snows from the countertop onto the kitchen floor. By the time Cameron joins us, a little dressing and a can of cranberries have transformed the commonest of poultry into the game we want.

Through Julian's eyes, we peer like bundled Londoners through the pop-up windows of *The Magic Toy Shop*, as we curl together on a throw rug to read aloud this Yuletide tale.

With an avid finger, Julian brings to life the major

figures. He sets the ballerina twirling on her string and, tugging on an arrow, marches the tin soldier toward her with a yearning heart. The lovers are cruelly parted for several frantic pages, yet . . . all ends happily.

None of us lives a single story—but an accumulation of stories past, and a simultaneity of present tales in varying stages. We may chafe through the tense climax of one, while expectantly introducing the characters in another. But how are we to blunt the power of those tales which must end tragically, if we don't cling to every victory? Until now, have I ever known how to revel in a happy ending?

Julian breaks my reverie—wasn't there another present? Watching our son's deft hands tear open the wrapping, unpacking and unpacking the outer doll and all the dolls within, I can't help but think we are too quick to seal our earlier lives inside us as we grow.

Out of our pride and shame at our progressions, we paint arresting emblems on our shells, while we make a tomb of the present in which to hide our antecedent selves. So blinded to our earlier designs, is it any wonder we can't decipher the cryptic meanings of our lives?

Julian lines the matryoshkas in an ascending row, then sets them spinning uproariously over the hardwood floor. I curb the urge to stop him. Tonight the picture's right somehow. Better to play with a nesting doll than to encase her.

As the dismantled figures twirl and rattle across the boards, I trade the painted icons on their bodices for recovered emblems of my own. Let this bodice bear the token of the pumpkin, that . . . the conch shell, this . . . the injured doll, that . . . the blackness, this . . . the snow.

But the deepest imprint on my heart is of this conjured holiday in November, when the toys we share are vivid symbols; and all the symbols that had once held court over me, at last, are only toys.

Epilogue

Through the mist of carbon-dioxide retention, her hands have forgotten nothing. Snapping her wrist, she slackens the yarn she draws from her invisible flying-swift, before she gives the warping reel another twirl.

"What are you making?" I lean down near her hospital gown to whisper.

"A lap shawl for you, Dear . . . since I have one."

"I know it will be beautiful," I tell her, and fall in love again, with Mother's hands.

A fit of coughing dispels her work, but only momentarily. In a tidy figure eight around her thumb and finger, lucent to the bone, she harmlessly wraps the cord of her oxygen, as if she were winding butterflies of wool.

Seeing her so content, I break away to check on Julian and Cam, still playing mancala in the waiting room. And then I telephone Jean-Paul. In twenty-seven years there's never been a zero hour in either of our lives that's gone unshared; so I tell him what I know of Mother's maladies—but this time hurriedly.

A prince of a young nurse lifts my mother's crooked body in his arms, while I smooth the fleece to ease the aching arc of her spine. A spark lights in her eyes as she entreats him, "Come back again, Dear, don't be long."

He sets her down, and sets her dreaming. Closing her eyes, she reaches toward the curtains only she can see, and draws them separately. "I'm in a castle," she confides in me so softly I need to put my ear to her lips. "I can't tell you now . . . but I will tomorrow. I'm going to a ball. There are veils between the rooms like gossamer, and everyone is . . . dressed so elegantly."

As if I would feel like Cinderella left behind, Mother takes my hand in one of hers and squeezes her apology for rushing off like this, without me.

I smile to think that she's been holding out on me for all these years—dutifully sharing with me her bitter disenchantment, when all it takes to revive her youthful dreams is a dashing figure, a handsome face.

Holding hands for what may be our last time, we wander off to separate lands. I am transported to China by a favorite fairy tale, "The Nightingale." A package arrives for the Emperor—a perfect clockwork bird, fashioned of gold and silver, inlaid with precious jewels. Dazzling without—and within, a cylinder for a heart. Its artificial song beguiles the Emperor.

And his gray little nightingale, no longer noticed, steals back to the woods with a throbbing throat, to sing out all he knows of happiness and sorrow.

Squeeze my hand, my ancient dreamer. But wish me no prince or palace, Mother—only the freedom of the nightingale to return now and then to the depths of my forest, and there to sing from my heart all that I've come to know of madness—and of love. ❖ ❖ ❖

Acknowledgments

I am deeply grateful to my sister Chris, without whose unwavering encouragement I would not have felt I could release *Legacy of Shadows*.

My husband Michael, always my source of good counsel, has lent his equilibrium during many anxious hours, throughout the several years of writing and producing this book. Our son Dave's insights, as well as his support for publishing this personal story, have meant more to me than he can know.

Legacy of Shadows could not have been written without our friend, and my life-long creative partner JP. How he maintained editorial distance on a story so near his own heart, through every draft from first to last, is a source of amazement to me. Whether sitting on the other side of this desk, or traveling around the world, he has been steadfastly accessible as my creative advisor.

To work again with Corasue Nicholas on the design of this second book, has felt like a fond homecoming. Once more I've counted heavily on her artistic judgment, her patience and flexibility.

Pam Livingston, a journalist whose early feedback on *Legacy* touched me so deeply, has sustained my determination to share this story. Her perceptive viewpoints and editorial skills lend a sense of grace to all she undertakes. It is a joy to work with her now on the presentation of this book.

Personal friends have given invaluable support and insightful critical feedback. In vivid memory are images of Paula Moore as I read to her each freshly finished section of *Legacy*. With shetland sheepdog Bailey on the couch beside her and ancient cat Duff in her lap, Paula listened with the intensity one dreams of in a reader. And when Susan Taylor was drawn to reread *Legacy of Shadows* three times during two very difficult days in her life, her account of its effect quelled the deep anxiety I felt just after deciding to release the book.

Two friends, with whom I've collaborated in

bringing stories to the stage as ballets, have individual-
ly and together enriched the book with the startling
insights that fellow artists in disciplines other than one's
own can provide. My thanks to Mim Eichmann,
choreographer, and Doug Lofstrom, composer.

To my agent Joe Durepos, who manages to main-
tain his deep convictions and values even in the harsh
world of publishing, I owe my appreciation for his
practical and spiritual support.

Many thanks to my attentive manuscript readers
for their helpful comments along the way: Betty Clegg,
Janet Dees, Zylphia Ford, Christopher Jocius, Pamela
Meiser, Dr. Robert Murphy, Randall Nicholas, and
Dorothy Parlow.

Helen Southgate Williams, who has been an
inspiration to me for four decades, has given *Legacy of
Shadows* the sort of blessing no one could give in her
stead.

And finally, my gratitude to Virginia Barry for
"what cannot be said with words."